DAMIEN PRESCOTT

Redemption Series, Book 4

SANDI LYNN

Sandi Lynn Romance

DAMIEN PRESCOTT

Redemption Series, Book 4

New York Times, USA Today & Wall Street Journal
Bestselling Author

Sandi Lynn

Damien Prescott

Cover Photo by Wander Aguia
Model: Forest H.
Cover Design by Shanoff Designs

Editing by BZ Hercules

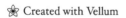 Created with Vellum

MISSION STATEMENT

Sandi Lynn Romance

Providing readers with romance novels that will whisk them away to another world and from the daily grind of life – one book at a time.

CHAPTER ONE

*D*amien

The morning sun filtered through the window as my alarm started buzzing. Reaching over, I grabbed my phone and sleepily turned it off. I gently removed the arm that was lying across my waist and climbed out of bed.

"You're leaving already?" she asked.

"Yeah. I have a plane to catch. You know this."

"We need to talk, Damien."

"Talk about what?"

I picked up my clothes that were on the floor and slipped into them. Sitting on the edge of the bed, I pulled on my socks and then my shoes.

"About us? You know I'm leaving for Italy tomorrow. I won't be here when you get back."

I stood up, grabbed my wallet from the dresser and tucked it into my back pocket. Picking up my watch, I looked at her while I put it on my wrist.

"Katherine, there is no us. I take you to dinner a couple times a week and we fuck. That's it. If you want to fuck some Italian guy over in Italy, be my guest. Now I have to go."

"You're a real fucking bastard, Damien Prescott."

"I never said I wasn't. Have a safe trip." I glanced at her one last time before walking out the door.

I hailed a cab to my 829 Park Ave penthouse and had the driver wait for me while I quickly packed a small bag. I'd be in Tennessee for two days. Short and sweet. In and out. My phone rang and it was my partner and best friend, Scott.

"Talk to me, Scott," I answered as I put him on speaker.

"I just emailed you the financials you asked for. Go get 'em, Damien."

"That's the plan. I'm not leaving there without a deal. Listen, I have to go. I'm running late for the airport."

"Good luck, man."

❧

*T*ennessee proved to be very profitable. I reeled the client in hook, line, and sinker. I was feeling good until I got to the airport to go home and found out my flight was delayed two hours.

"What the fuck." I sighed. I needed to get back. I had business to attend to. I pulled my phone from my suit coat and dialed my secretary, Joslyn.

"Hello, Mr. Prescott."

"Joslyn, my flight has been delayed for two hours and I'm stuck in this miserable airport. I need you to push back my meeting to two o'clock."

"I'll call Mr. Cannon right now and tell him."

I pushed the end button and slipped my phone back in my pocket. I looked around for the nearest coffee place and found one. It was too damn early for this shit. I stood in the long line and not with much patience. Patience wasn't a friend of mine. In fact, we were enemies. Up ahead, there was a woman standing in line who was next. Certainly she would let me cut in. I stepped out of line and walked in front of her.

"Excuse me. Do you mind if I cut in front you? I'm in a hurry," I asked as politely as I knew how while I stared into her big deep blue eyes; eyes that looked like the waters that flowed into the pristine white sand beaches.

"No, of course not." She smiled. "Go right ahead."

"Hey, thanks."

My turn. I walked up to the counter and ordered my coffee. Black and strong. I needed something to wake me the fuck up, since celebrating last night with the new client had extended into the wee hours of the morning. I paid, and the barista set my coffee down on the counter. I picked it up and took one last look at the woman with the big blue eyes.

"I appreciate it." I held up my cup and walked away.

"You could have at least bought my coffee since I let you cut in front of me," I heard her shout. "That would have been a gentleman-like thing to do."

"Bitch," I mumbled.

But there was no doubt she was one hell of a beautiful bitch. My phone rang and when I pulled it out of my pocket, I saw it was Scott calling.

"What's up, Scott?" I asked as I headed to my gate.

"I don't want to make your morning any shittier than it already is, but we lost the Coleman account."

"What the fuck happened?" I yelled a little too loudly.

"Apparently, he had a run in with Adam and the two of them got into it. He fired the firm on the spot."

"That fucking little prick. I want his ass fired and out of my building before I land in New York. Do you understand me? That is the last straw with him."

"I figured you'd say that. You want me to fire him?"

"No. I'll do it myself over the phone. Call security and have them on standby."

I ended the call and quickly dialed Adam.

"Listen, Damien, I can explain," he quickly answered.

"No explanation needed, Adam. You're fired. Do you understand me? Done! Get the fuck out of my building now!"

"There's two sides to every story, Damien. You're not even going to listen to me?"

"I've listened to you enough. I warned you if it happened again, you were out. It happened, you're out."

I ended the call and dialed Scott.

"That was fast," he answered.

"Get security up there and have them escort him out."

"I'll do it now," he spoke.

I sighed and placed my phone in my pocket. I reached my gate and took a seat to try and calm down.

"You were in such a hurry to wait for a flight that is delayed two hours?" the woman from the coffee line asked with a narrowed eye as she stood in front of me.

Great.

"Yeah. I have work to do. I didn't have time to stand in that ridiculous line. And since you're here, standing in front of me, giving me the evil eye, I didn't appreciate your comment back there."

"I'm not sorry I said it. Have you ever heard of paying it forward? It's a good way to live your life." She smiled.

I couldn't believe this crazy woman, and I wasn't in the mood.

"I've heard of it. It's my choice and I chose not to. Now if you'll excuse me, I have work to do. Please remove yourself from my view."

She walked away and I couldn't help but watch. Five foot six, approximately 120 lbs., shoulder-length blonde hair that held perky waves, black leggings, an oversized light pink sweater that clung to her perfectly shaped ass and black boots that hit right below the knee. She was definitely a looker, and a crazy one at that. Shit.

CHAPTER TWO

*L*ondon

"Jerk," I mumbled to myself as I walked away.

It didn't matter that he was hot, like the hottest guy I'd seen in a long time. Six foot two, nice build, short dark hair, five o'clock shadow, deep brown eyes, designer suit. Uptight, cocky, rude, arrogant, egotistical, no respect. I overheard his phone conversation. Who couldn't? The impression I got was that he was all business all the time and that his life was nothing but work. I had a gift for reading people and I was never wrong. Since I had some time to kill, I decided to grab a bite to eat. Tootsie's Orchid Lounge was near my gate and it was pretty crowded, but I managed to get the only small table they had left. I ordered my breakfast, and as I was waiting, I saw that rude man arguing with the hostess about something.

"Hey." I waved.

He glanced at me and walked over to my table.

"You're more than welcome to sit at my table," I said. "It is the only available seat in the place."

"Breakfast with you?" His brow arched.

"If you're hungry, sit down."

His eye steadily narrowed at me for a moment.

"No thanks. You'll expect something in return." He turned and walked away.

I rolled my eyes and pulled out my phone. After I finished eating, I figured I better use the restroom before boarding the plane. There was a line, so I stood and waited. After I was finished, I walked to my gate and noticed they had already started boarding. I got in line, waited my turn, and then boarded the plane. *Oh no. Dear god no.* He looked up from his phone as I sat down next to him.

"Oh hell no. You're on this flight?"

"Yes." I smiled.

"In first class?"

"Yes. Would you like to see my ticket? When I checked in, they gave me a free upgrade. I was supposed to be in the main cabin."

"Of course they did." He sighed and went back to looking at his phone.

I ignored him and began talking to the older woman that sat in the aisle seat across from me. We chatted about her family, astrology and her jewelry business. She handmade jewelry and was in Tennessee selling her pieces at a jewelry show.

"May I?" She extended her hand to me.

"For fuck sakes." I heard the man next to me mumble.

I gently placed my hand in hers as her fingers wrapped tightly around mine. She looked at me and her eyes widened while a hint of tears started to form.

"It's okay," I whispered as I gave her a small heartfelt smile.

She let go of my hand, reached into her bag, and pulled out a beautiful silver chain. Attached to the chain was a charm: a circle with a picture of the Tree of Life engraved on it.

"I want you to have this, dear."

"It's beautiful, but I can't accept this for free. Let me pay you something."

"No. That won't be necessary. Just your kindness was payment enough. May you grow stronger and continue striving for greater knowledge and the new experiences you are seeking."

"That's so sweet of you. Thank you."

"You're welcome. I'm going to take a nap for a short while. We'll chat later." She smiled.

I put the necklace around my neck and traced the outline of the tree with my fingers.

"Okay, that was weird," the man next to me spoke.

"What was?"

"Who the hell just randomly gives a total stranger something like that?"

"A nice person who cares about others," I spoke.

"Whatever. Anyway, I overheard you tell her that you came to Tennessee to see Graceland and the Grand Ole Opry?"

"Yes." I smiled.

"Why?" His brows furrowed. "That sounds utterly boring."

"It wasn't. It was an experience." I laughed. "Plus, I like Elvis Presley and a lot of the old country music."

"Okay, then." His brows raised like he was repulsed as he looked back down at his phone.

"You know what's sad?" I asked.

"If I don't say what, I have a feeling you're going to tell me anyway."

"It's sad that your work is your life and it consumes you to the point that you don't notice anything around you."

"Excuse me?" He looked at me.

"Never mind."

"No. I won't never mind. What the hell do you mean by that?" he angrily asked.

"I can just tell you're a workaholic and your work consumes your life."

"Damn right it does. Where there's money to be made, you go after it. I love my job and it makes me a lot of money."

"Is that what's important to you?"

"Of course. Who the hell doesn't like or want money? Isn't money what paid for your little fantasy trip to Tennessee?"

"Yes. But it shouldn't be the only and most important thing in your life."

"Well, it is. I need to get back to my emails, so please stop talking."

I rolled my eyes and took my laptop out of my bag. Opening up my Word document, I began to write about my Tennessee adventures. I could see him out of the corner of my eye stealing glances at what I was writing.

"I'm writing about my trip," I spoke.

"And? Why are you telling me?"

"Because I saw you looking."

"No I wasn't."

"It's okay." I smiled at him. "I know you're curious."

"I am not curious. To be honest, I could care less."

I was really starting to think that this man was the most awful person I'd ever met. The plane finally landed in New York, and I was on to my next adventure. I stood up and let him get out first.

"I know you're in a hurry to go yell at some more people, so please, you go first." I motioned with my hand.

He shot me a look.

"I can't say it's been a pleasure flying with you," he spoke.

"The pleasure was all mine, sir." I grinned.

He shook his head and exited the plane. I looked over and noticed his wallet was sitting in the seat. Shit. I grabbed it and tried to push my way through the people who cut in front of me.

"Excuse me. I need to get off right away. The man next to me left his wallet. Excuse me," I said as I squeezed through.

I ran as fast as I could down the boarding bridge. When I finally made it into the airport, I looked around. I didn't see him. Baggage claim. Yes! That was where he'd be. I followed the signs to baggage claim. I had no idea where I was going because I'd never been to this airport or New York before. Found it. I looked around and didn't see him. Looking up on the screen, I saw which carousel our luggage was going to be on. I ran over and he wasn't there. The luggage hadn't been loaded yet as passengers from the plane stood and patiently waited. Perhaps he didn't check a bag. I sighed as I held the wallet in my hand. Tossing it in my purse, I grabbed my suitcase when it came around and left the airport.

CHAPTER THREE

*D*amien

    I climbed into the back of the cab and took it to the office. When the driver pulled up to the building, I reached in my pocket and noticed my wallet wasn't there.

"What the fuck?" I spoke in a panic.

Reaching into my coat pocket, I pulled out the credit card I had stuck in there with my license and paid the cab driver. Great. This was just great. What the fuck else was going to go wrong today? I angrily grabbed my bag, exited the cab, and walked into the building. I was fuming. My money, credit cards, expense receipts, and more were in that wallet. Taking the elevator up to the fifth floor, I stormed out and into my office.

"Joslyn," I yelled. "Get in here!"

"Yes, Mr. Prescott?" she nervously asked.

"I need you to call the airport and see if anyone turned in my wallet. If not, I need you to cancel all my credit cards."

"You lost your wallet?"

"I think it might have fallen out of my pocket on the plane. Call them now!"

"Yes, sir."

Just as Joslyn was walking out, Scott walked in.

"Welcome back to the Big Apple." He grinned and I snarled. "What was that for? You still pissed off about Adam?"

"That was the trip from hell. First off, I got stuck next to this annoying beautiful woman."

"I can see how that can be a problem." He rolled his eyes.

"It was a problem. She was fucking nuts. I feel sorry for her boyfriend if she has one. If she doesn't, I can see why. And, I lost my wallet. I think I left it on the plane."

"Oh shit. That's not cool, Damien."

"Joslyn is calling the airport to see if anyone turned it in. But it's highly unlikely. Even if they did, I'm sure they stole all the cash I had in it. You know, that woman went to Tennessee to visit Graceland and The Grand Ole Opry."

"So? A lot of people do that," he said.

"It's just weird. And then the lady across the aisle from her gave her some necklace she hand made. She doesn't even know her. Do you believe she had the nerve to tell me that money shouldn't be the only important thing in life? And she said I was a workaholic who let my work consume me."

"Well, you are a workaholic and you do nothing but work 24/7."

"And? What's your point?"

"I'm just saying. By the way, you sure are getting all worked up over this woman. Why?"

"I am not. I'm just saying she was annoying and wouldn't stop talking to me. I asked her for one favor and it was all downhill from there."

"What favor was that?" He smiled.

"The line at the coffee shop was too long, so I asked her if I could cut in front of her because I was in a hurry."

"You were in a hurry to sit and wait for your delayed flight?" He laughed.

"The point is I didn't have the patience to stand in line. Anyway, she let me and then had the nerve to say that I should have bought her coffee since she let me cut in front of her."

"That actually would have been a nice thing to do."

"Get out of here, Scott."

"No. This woman really affected you and I want to know why."

"Because everywhere I turned, there she was. It was so damn annoying. It was bad enough I had to deal with her in the airport, then come to find out she had the seat right next to me. The airline upgraded her for free. Do you believe that? Just my luck. Now my wallet is missing."

"And don't forget that you had to fire Adam."

"Yeah. That too."

He stood there and narrowed his eye at me for a moment.

"Mr. Prescott?" Joslyn popped her head through the door. "The airport said no one has turned in a wallet."

"Of course not. They're probably too busy using all my credit cards!" I shouted. "Cancel them now!"

CHAPTER FOUR

London

 I was sitting in the back of the cab when I opened his wallet. It was stuffed with cash and a couple of credit cards. I didn't see a driver's license, so I pulled out one of his business cards: **Damien Prescott CEO, The Prescott Group, 276 5th Avenue, New York, NY.**

"Where to, lady?" the cab driver asked.

"276 5th Avenue, please."

Was this a coincidence? I was doing a freelance project for the Prescott Group. The driver pulled up to the curb.

"Can you wait for me, please? I just have to drop this wallet off and then I'll need you to take me to my Airbnb."

"Of course." He kindly smiled.

I entered the building and the doorman asked if I needed help.

"I'm looking for the Prescott Group," I spoke.

"Take the elevator up to the fifth floor. Someone will be there to help you when you get off."

"Thank you." I smiled.

I took the elevator up to the fifth floor. I wasn't looking forward to seeing that rude man again and prayed he had gone home from the airport. That was wishful thinking on my part. He needed his wallet, and the very little I knew about him, I was sure he was in an uproar over losing it.

"Can I help you?" a nice redheaded woman asked as I stepped out of the elevator.

"I'm looking for Damien Prescott."

"I'm sorry, but Mr. Prescott is busy. Is there something I can help you with?"

"I found his wallet." I held it up.

"Oh. Thank god. He's been a tyrant ever since he got back. Go down the hallway and make a right. His office is at the end. You can give it to his secretary, Joslyn."

"Thank you." I smiled.

I walked down the hallway all the way to the end and made a right. The moment I turned the corner, I saw a desk with a nameplate on it that said "Joslyn" and a woman in her mid-forties with sandy-brown shoulder-length hair sitting behind it on the phone. She stared at me with a look on her face I couldn't quite describe.

"Give me a moment," she whispered as she held up her finger.

I held Damien's wallet up and her eyes widened. She quickly hung up the phone.

"Is that—"

"Yes. This is Mr. Prescott's wallet. He left it in his seat on the airplane."

"God bless you, honey. Did you have to sit next to him?" she asked in a whisper.

"Yes."

"I'm so sorry."

All of a sudden, his office door opened.

"Joslyn," he shouted. "What the hell?" He looked at me and his eyes widened. "You. Are you fucking stalking me?"

"In all honesty, I couldn't stalk you because I didn't even know your name. So how would I stalk you?" I held up his wallet. "You left this in your seat."

"My wallet."

I handed it to him, and he quickly opened it and counted his cash.

"It's all there, Mr. Prescott. Trust me, I'm not interested in your money and I'm not a thief."

"You can never be too careful these days," he calmly spoke. "You went out of your way to bring this to me?"

"Yes. I knew you must have been freaking out. Plus, I wanted to spare the poor souls in this office who work for you."

I heard a snicker come from Joslyn.

He held his finger up and pursed his lips together.

"Thank you," he finally spoke.

"You're welcome. I hope the rest of your day goes better, Mr. Prescott." I turned and walked away.

I climbed into the cab and thanked the driver for waiting for me.

"Where to?" he asked.

I pulled up the email on my phone.

"525 West 28th Street, please."

I stepped inside my new studio Airbnb that would be my home for one month. I rolled my suitcase into the bedroom and then looked around the small space. It was beautifully decorated in a mix of light and dark grays. Walking over to the window in the living room, I stared out at the city that I'd always dreamed of seeing. I let out a long yawn and my eyes felt heavy. It had been an exhausting day already and I needed to take a nap before I ventured out into the big city.

CHAPTER FIVE

*D*amien

It was ten o'clock before I finally left the office and headed home. I stepped into my penthouse, turned on the lights and went to my room to change into something more comfortable. Walking to the kitchen, I opened the refrigerator and pulled out a carton of leftover chicken teriyaki, scooped it on a plate, and threw it in the microwave. Once it was done reheating, I took it over to the table, where I set down my laptop and began working while I ate. The thing was, I couldn't focus. The only thing that kept running around in my head were the events of today and that girl. The one who let me cut in front of her in line. The one who offered me to sit with her for breakfast. The one with the big smile, and no matter what I said to her, that smile never left her face. The same girl who went out of her way to bring me my wallet. My phone dinged, and when I looked at it, there was a text message from Katherine.

"Just in case you were wondering, I made it to Italy, asshole."

I rolled my eyes and didn't respond. There was no need to. I really didn't care. The only thing I cared about in life was my business, money and how to make more. I was already at the top at the age of thirty, but I wanted to be higher. I wanted more.

*T*he next morning, I was sitting at my desk when Landon from the graphics department walked in.

"Morning, Damien. I need your approval on these."

"What is it?"

"The mock-ups for the Stafford account."

"Just leave them on my desk. I'll look at them later. I'm busy right now."

"But—"

"What part did you not understand?" I snapped at him. "I said I'll look at them later!"

"Yeah. Sure. Sorry." He walked out of my office.

"Hey, Landon just said you're in a mood." Scott smiled as he stepped into my office. "I asked him what else was new."

"Very funny. Don't forget we have that dinner meeting tonight with Bradbury."

"How could I forget. You are bringing Katherine, right?"

"Katherine is in Italy and I'm not seeing her anymore."

"Bro, then you better get that little black book of yours out and find someone. You know Bradbury is a family man and he wants a company that's family oriented. He specifically said he hates these bigshots that only care about business. Which, my friend, is you. You need to show up with a hot chick on your arm or else we're going to lose this deal. I don't know about you, but I think securing a multi-million-dollar account is worth faking it for one night."

"Shit." I leaned back in my chair. "Don't worry. I'll make a couple calls. With everything going on, I forgot. I'm going to grab a cup of coffee," I said as I got up from my chair.

"Why? You always have Joslyn get it for you."

"I need the walk. I didn't sleep well last night."

He looked at his watch. "I have to go. I'm meeting Madison for a quick breakfast."

We walked out of my office together. He went right and I went left and headed to the break room for a cup of coffee. On my way back, I heard the elevator ding, and when I happened to look up, I saw that girl from the plane step off. *What the fuck?*

"Considering I didn't leave anything else behind, I'm going to say you're stalking me now," I spoke as I walked up to her.

"Good morning." She brightly smiled. "You can stop flattering yourself. I'm just here to drop something off. Have a good day, Mr. Prescott." She turned and pressed the button to the elevator.

"Excuse me? What the hell would you have to drop off here? At my company?"

The elevator doors opened and she stepped inside.

"The artwork for one of your accounts."

The doors closed and I stood there in confusion for a moment before I went over to the elevator and pressed the button.

"Damn it," I spoke, as it was taking too long.

I took the stairs down to the lobby and rushed out the door, looking to see which way she went. She wasn't too far down, so I ran to catch up with her.

"Hold on a second. You need to explain to me what the hell just happened back there."

"What's to explain? Your company hired me to do some freelance work and I was dropping it off. I finished it last night," she said as she kept walking.

"For fuck sakes, will you stop for a minute?"

She stopped and turned to me.

"What?"

"None of this is making any sense to me at all. First we meet at the airport and now you're doing freelance work for my company?"

"Yeah. Weird. Right?" She smiled.

I took in a deep breath to try and calm myself.

"Come back to my office with me. I want to know exactly who you are," I spoke in a stern tone.

"Say 'please.'"

"Excuse me?"

"Say 'please' and I'll go back with you. There's a right way and a wrong way to ask."

I was two seconds away from losing my shit.

"Will you *please* come back to my office with me?"

"Sure. Now didn't that feel better asking politely?"

We walked back to the building and took the elevator up to the fifth floor. As we stepped out of the elevator, I grabbed the envelope she left at the front desk and we headed to my office.

"Joslyn, hold all my calls."

"Yes, Mr. Prescott."

"Hi, Joslyn." She smiled.

"Good morning. It's nice to see you again," Joslyn spoke.

Shutting the door, I told her to take a seat as I sat down behind my desk.

"First of all, what is your name?" I asked.

"London Everly."

"London?" I arched my brow.

"I was conceived in London. My mom thought it was cute."

"Oh. How did you end up doing work for us?"

"I was contacted by Jeff, one of your employees, who saw my work on a website."

"So why the hell didn't you say anything yesterday when you brought me my wallet?"

"To be honest, Mr. Prescott, you really didn't want to hear anything I had to say."

I sighed, leaned back in my chair, and stared at her.

"Is something wrong?" she asked. "I'm not sure I like the way you're staring at me."

"No. I'm just trying to figure you out. Have you lived in New York your whole life?"

"I don't live here. Actually, this is my first time in New York. I'm staying for about a month and then I'm leaving."

"Where are you from?"

"Minnesota."

"And why are you here and only for a month?" I asked out of curiosity.

"I have things I want to see and experience, and a month is all I'll need."

"Like what?" I narrowed my eye at her.

"Just the sights New York has to offer," she replied.

I needed to know more about her because she was the most bizarre, annoying beautiful girl I'd ever met.

I ran my hand through my hair as I couldn't believe what I was about to do.

"You know, I'm actually glad I ran into you. Do you know anyone in New York?"

"No." She shook her head.

"Now that's not true, London. You know me. Since I'm the only person you know here, I'm asking you for a favor."

"A favor?" She cocked her head. "What could I possibly do for you?"

"Attend a business dinner with me tonight."

She let out a light laugh.

"You," she pointed at me, "want me," she pointed to herself, "to go to a business dinner with you?"

"Yes."

"First of all, Mr. Prescott, I don't know you. We exchanged some words, and not too pleasant ones on your end, in an airport in Nashville and then again on the plane where you told me to stop talking. Second of all, what are you after?"

"I'm not after anything. Listen." I sighed. "I have a very important meeting with a potential client and he's all about family and shit. He only deals with firms that are basically the same. So I need to bring someone to make it look like I believe in the same shit he does. I can't show up alone or I'll lose the deal."

"But why me? I'm sure you have a harem, a tribe of women at your beck and call."

"I do." I grinned. "But it's short notice and you're here, so I'm asking you. It saves me the trouble of having to find someone. Which to be honest, I don't have time for. Do me this favor and you will be well compensated."

"I don't want your money, Mr. Prescott. Not everything or everyone can be bought." She got up from her seat. "Thank you for the invite, but I'm going to have to decline." She began to walk towards the door, and I stood up from my seat.

"London, please. Please come with me tonight."

She stopped, turned around, and stared at me for a moment.

"This is really important to you, isn't it?"

"It is. It's a huge deal and one I'm not willing to lose over something as stupid as family and values."

"Fine. I'll go with you on one condition," she spoke.

"What's your condition?" I narrowed my eye at her.

"You take me to the Empire State Building tomorrow."

"Seriously? You want to go there? Why?" I frowned.

"Why not?" She smiled.

"Sure. Okay. I'll take you to the Empire State Building."

"Thank you, and I'll go with you tonight. What time?"

"Dinner is at seven thirty, so I'll pick you up at six forty-five? Which hotel are you staying at?"

"I'm not. I'm staying at an Airbnb on West 28th Street."

"Text me the address," I spoke.

"Are you sure you want to give me your phone number?" she asked.

"Do I have a choice?" I arched my brow at her.

She pulled her phone from her bag and I rattled off my number.

"Sent," she spoke. "I'll see you tonight, Mr. Prescott." She opened the door and walked out of my office.

CHAPTER SIX

*D*amien

"Who the hell was that beauty that just walked out of here?" Scott smiled as he stepped inside.

"I thought you were at breakfast."

"We only had time to grab a quick bagel. Madison got called into an emergency court hearing. Again, who was that beauty?"

"Her name is London Everly and she's the woman from the airport, the plane, and the one who returned my wallet to me."

"Fuck, Damien. You weren't kidding when you said she was beautiful. What was she doing here? Is she stalking you or something?" He laughed.

"So get this," I leaned across my desk, "she was hired by Jeff to do some freelance work for us. She was dropping off the artwork." I handed him the envelope.

"Wow. She's good. I can see why Jeff hired her. But wait." He shook his head. "So she knew when she returned your wallet yesterday that she was doing freelance work for us?"

"Yep. She sure did and she didn't say a damn word about it. When I confronted her and asked her why she didn't tell me, her response was, 'You really didn't want to hear what I had to say.' Do you believe that?"

"Yeah." He nodded his head. "Actually, I do."

I rolled my eyes and sighed as I leaned back in my chair.

"She's coming to dinner with us tonight."

"What?" He laughed. "How the hell did you manage that?"

"It saves me the trouble of trying to find someone. She was here, so I took advantage. The only problem is, she said she'd go with me on one condition."

"What's that?" He smiled.

"She wants me to take her to the Empire State Building tomorrow. Supposedly, this is her first time in New York and she's only going to be here a month."

"Tourists." He shook his head. "So I assume you're taking her?"

"Nah. I just told her I would. I'll bail out tomorrow morning."

"Bro, that's really being an asshole. She's doing you a favor tonight. The least you can do is take her to the Empire State Building."

"The answer is no, my friend. I just need her for tonight and then I don't have any plans to see her again."

"Why? She's smoking hot."

"You're right, she is, but she's really off. She's strange and overly nice. Plus, she seems like the type that would get attached really easy. I don't need that shit."

"My bad. I didn't think being nice was a turn-off," he spoke. "And even if she did get attached, she's only here for a month."

"Doesn't matter. My luck, she'd permanently move here."

"Alright." He sighed. "I have to go. I'll talk to you later. I cannot wait to see how this unfolds tonight." He grinned before walking out of my office.

❦

*T*he car pulled up to her apartment building, and when I stepped inside, I took the elevator up to the seventh floor. As I stepped off the elevator and went to knock on her door, a young woman in the next apartment walked out.

"Hi." She smiled.

"Umm. Hi."

"So you're the one taking London to dinner tonight." She grinned as she looked me up and down.

"I'm taking her to a business dinner. It's not a date or anything."

"Didn't say it was." She smiled. "Consider yourself lucky. She's awesome."

I narrowed my eye at her and slowly shook my head.

"How do you even know her? She just got here yesterday."

"We met on the elevator this morning and I invited her in for coffee. She's awesome."

"Yes. You already said that," I spoke.

"I have to run. Have fun on your date."

"It's not a date. She's doing me a favor," I shouted as she walked away.

Suddenly, the door opened and I swallowed hard as London stood before me. She was dressed in a black dress with three-quarter-length sleeves and a small slit up the side. Her hair was straight compared to the wavy look I'd previously seen her with. She was stunning.

"I thought I heard you talking to someone," she spoke.

"Your neighbor." I pointed.

"Oh. You met Sharlene? She's so sweet. We had coffee this morning after I got back from your office."

"Yeah. She felt the need to tell me."

"Come on in. I just have to grab my purse."

I stepped inside and looked around. I was actually shocked she was staying in something so nice.

"Nice place you have here," I spoke.

"Thanks. The pictures online really don't do it justice. I'm ready." She grinned.

We walked out of the building and climbed into the back of the town car I had rented.

"Fancy, Mr. Prescott." She smiled.

I gave her a small smile and then went over the rules for the night.

"There are a few things I need to go over with you and I want you to listen to me very carefully. We're having dinner with Don Bradbury, CEO of Bradbury Meats Ltd. His company is worth billions."

"I know Bradbury meats," she spoke.

"Good. He prides himself on being a family man. His company is run by all of his family. He's been married for thirty years and has six children. Family is everything to him and when he found out that the ad executive at his former ad agency was getting divorced because he cheated on his wife of ten years, he dropped them immediately. He's a very Christian man and goes to church every Sunday. So I need you to just go with the flow tonight. Don't talk. I'll do the talking. You just sit there and smile."

"You do know that you're lying, right?" she asked.

"Yeah. And? It's a multi-million-dollar account. A little white lie isn't going to hurt anyone."

"I'm really excited to see the Empire State Building tomorrow." A smile crossed her lips.

"Why? So you came all the way to New York for that?"

"And other things."

"Like?" I asked with an arch in my brow.

"I want to see every part of Central Park, the Statue of Liberty, Rockefeller Center, a Broadway play, the art museum, Times Square at night, Grand Central Station, and a few other places."

The car pulled up to Grammercy Tavern and I climbed out first. The driver walked around and helped London out of the car.

"Thank you." She smiled at him.

When we walked inside, Scott and Madison were already seated.

"There he is." Scott smiled.

"Hey, Scott. Hello, Madison. I'd like you both to meet London Everly. London, this is my friend and partner, Scott, and his wife, Madison."

"It's nice to meet you, London." Scott smiled as he gently shook her hand.

"What a beautiful name," Madison spoke. "It's nice to meet you."

"It's a pleasure to meet both of you," London spoke with a grin on her face as we took our seats."

God, I prayed she could pull this off. The reason she came to New York was to sightsee. There was no way being a freelance artist she could afford to travel the way she did. Something was up with her and I was going to find out what it was.

CHAPTER SEVEN

*L*ondon
   Damien Prescott looked incredibly sexy in his black suit, white dress shirt, and black and purple tie. I only agreed to go to his business dinner because there was something about him that drew me in. Maybe it was his rudeness or his mean nature. But I believed that, deep down, there was a good man inside him. He was a man who was addicted to his work and didn't appreciate life that was around him. He was conceited, arrogant, and just an overall dick, but something told me that it was all a façade. All he needed was some time away from his demanding work schedule to see what life was really about and what really mattered most. I had a small thought that maybe while I was in New York, I could help him.

"So, London, I don't see a ring on that pretty little finger yet." Mr. Bradbury smiled. "What are you waiting for, Damien?" he asked him.

Damien chuckled.

"We are definitely talking about it. She knows she's the love of my life and I can't live without her. Isn't that right, sweetheart?"

"Yes." I brightly smiled. "We're just waiting for the perfect time."

"There is no perfect time," Mr. Bradbury spoke. "How many kids do the two of you want?"

Damien glanced over at me.

"Four." I grinned. "A nice even number."

"Four is an excellent number." Mr. Bradbury beamed. "Dana and I planned on four and just when we thought we were done, two more surprised us. But it was God's will that we bring six children into the world. Who were we to argue?" He let out a jolly laugh.

"Yes, you can't argue with God's will." I smiled. "When he has a plan, there's nothing in the world that you can do to stop it. What's meant to be is meant to be."

"That's right, young lady." Mr. Bradbury held up his glass. "You've got a real keeper, Damien. I suggest you hurry up and put a ring on that pretty little finger of hers before someone swoops by and snatches her away from you."

Damien gave him an uncomfortable smile.

"Don't worry about that, Don. I plan on it."

Dinner was over and we said our goodbyes to Don and his wife, Scott and Madison. Climbing into the back of the car, Damien shut the door and let out a deep breath.

"You did good, London. Thanks. I love how you threw in the part about God. That was a nice touch."

"It's true."

"Yeah. Okay." He rolled his eyes. "Anyway, I better get you home. It's late. By the way, I'll have to meet you at the Empire State Building tomorrow. Say around eleven?"

"Sure. That's fine."

"I have a meeting early in the morning."

"On a Saturday?" I asked.

"Yes. Regardless of what day it is, my work doesn't stop."

I had a feeling inside me. The same feeling I always got when I knew a guy was lying to me. He said he'd meet me at the Empire State Building at eleven, but I knew, deep down, he wasn't going to show at all. I'd get a text message around ten forty-five from him saying his meeting was running late and he wasn't sure what time it would end.

"You work too much." I politely smiled.

"So you've told me before," he spoke.

The driver pulled up to my apartment building and Damien

climbed out first so I could get out. He held out his hand to help me from the car and I refused it.

"I can get out myself. Thank you for dinner. I'll see you tomorrow." I casually smiled and walked away.

"London?" I heard him call my name before I stepped into the building.

I turned around and looked at him as he stood by the car.

"Thanks again for tonight."

I gave him a small smile and a nod as I walked inside and went up to my apartment.

*

The next morning, I climbed out of bed, let out a long yawn, and headed to the kitchen to make some coffee. Leaning over the counter as I waited for my coffee to finish brewing, I thought about how excited I was to see the Empire State Building. To some, it was no big deal, but to me, it meant the world. Even if Damien didn't show, I wouldn't let it ruin my day. It was probably best he didn't come anyway because I didn't need his comments and negativity. Being physically alone in the world was something I was used to and being alone was how it had to be. I did, however, have friends all around the world. People who followed my blog and my journey. Five hundred thousand to be exact.

After finishing my coffee, I took a shower, got dressed, and headed to the Empire State Building. When I arrived, it was ten fifty. At ten fifty-five, a text message came through from Damien.

"I'm sorry, but I'm still stuck in this meeting. Not sure how long it's going to last. Maybe another time."

"No worries. I didn't expect you to come anyway. Have a great day."

"What do you mean you didn't expect me to come?"

I smiled as I read his last message and tucked my phone into my purse. Life would go on without Mr. Damien Prescott in it. I took in everything the Empire State Building had to offer. As I stood on the 86th floor observation deck, I looked out at the huge city as a feeling of peace washed over me. Life was happening all around me and the only thing I could do was smile at it all.

"Pretty cool, eh?" a man who was one of the uniformed personnel asked as he stood next to me.

"It is." I smiled as I glanced over at him.

"First time here?" he asked.

"Yeah. It is."

"You haven't seen anything until you see it at night. Come back after ten p.m. You'll be happy you did."

"Thank you. I will." I smiled.

"Have a nice day, ma'am." He tipped his hat.

"You too."

I spent a total of three hours there exploring and taking pictures. Before heading out, I grabbed some lunch and then a coffee from Starbucks. When I reached the streets of the city, I pulled my phone from my purse and noticed I had three text messages from Damien.

"Hello?"

"Why didn't you respond to my question?"

"London, this is very rude not to text me back."

I couldn't help but laugh. He was calling *me* rude?

"Mr. Prescott, I just left the Empire State Building. I was there to see the sights, not be on my phone. Priorities. And replying to your text message wasn't a top one."

"Seriously? Are you serious? It's called common courtesy."

"Are you being hypocritical right now? Because I believe you don't reply to half the women who text you."

He didn't respond and I hailed a cab back to my apartment. When I stepped off the elevator, I stopped halfway down the hall when I saw Damien standing in front of my door.

I sighed.

"Damien, what are you doing here?" I asked as I slid the key into the lock.

"I came to have a little chat with you because I don't particularly like your attitude."

I let out a light laugh as I stood there with my hand on the doorknob.

"You think this is funny? I don't put up with women talking to me the way you do."

"And I don't put up with lying men either. So please do us both a favor and move along."

I opened the door, and when I stepped inside, my feet were covered in water.

"What the hell!" I exclaimed as I looked down. "Oh my God."

"What the hell is right," Damien spoke as he looked down at the carpet. "It looks like you had a flood. Did you leave the water running or the washer on?"

"No! Nothing was on when I left."

I walked further into the apartment while Damien stood outside in the hallway. I looked around and found the entire apartment was flooded.

"If you're just going to stand there and watch, I suggest you leave," I spoke with irritation.

"Fine. We'll talk about this another time."

He began to walk away, and I slowly shook my head.

"Shit," he spoke as he took off his shoes and walked into the apartment.

"I thought you left."

"Be quiet please," he said as he looked around. "It looks like a pipe burst. You better call the people you're renting from right now."

I pulled my phone from my purse, called the lady I was renting from, and explained to her what happened. She told me to hang tight and that she was calling the building manager right away.

"London?" I heard Sharlene call from the doorway. "Oh my god, it happened to you too. I just got home and my apartment is flooded."

"The building manager is on his way up." I sighed.

"This happened a few years ago and I had to move into a hotel for two months," she spoke. "I can't go through that again."

Russ, the building manager, walked into the apartment wearing tall rubber boots.

"Damn it." He shook his head. "I know you're renting this place from Carly, and I'm sorry to say you're going to have to collect your things and leave."

"For how long?" I asked.

"I really can't say. The last time this happened, it took about two months to get the apartments cleaned and restored."

"Okay. I'll go grab my suitcase. Good thing I haven't unpacked yet."

It was also a good thing that I had my suitcase lying across a lounge chair in the bedroom. I went into the bathroom and collected some personal items, threw them in my suitcase, and zipped it shut.

"Damien, can you please carry this for me?" I shouted from the bedroom. "I don't want to wheel it in all that water and it's quite heavy."

He walked into the bedroom, picked up my suitcase, and carried it to the hallway.

"Thank you," I said.

"Where are you going to go?" Sharlene asked.

"I don't know. I guess I'll have to find a hotel for a couple nights and look for a new Airbnb to rent."

"Why can't she stay with you?" Sharlene asked Damien with a narrowed eye and her hand on her hip.

"With me?" he asked with surprise as he pointed to himself.

"Yeah. I'm sure you live in some fancy schmancy penthouse with an extra bedroom or five. After all, she did do you a favor last night." She bopped her head from side to side. "Now it's your turn to repay the favor. It's called paying it forward."

CHAPTER EIGHT

*D*amien
            What the fuck was with these people and their paying it forward?

I couldn't believe this woman. The nerve of her. Who the hell did she think she was?

"Sharlene, it's okay," London spoke as she placed her hand on her arm. "I'll be okay. This is just a little setback, nothing I can't figure out. Trust me, this is nothing compared to what I've been through."

London gave her one last hug and started heading towards the elevator. I followed behind.

"Where are you going to go?" I asked.

"I don't know yet. When I get down to the lobby, I'll look up some hotels on my phone."

We reached the lobby and she took a seat in one of the chairs and started typing away on her phone.

"I guess I'm going to go. Good luck with everything," I spoke.

"Thank you. I appreciate it." She softly smiled at me.

I took in a deep breath, tucked my hands in my pants pockets, and walked out of the building. While I stood at the curb and signaled for a cab, I couldn't stop this gnawing feeling inside me. I didn't need this.

My mind kept remembering what she said to Sharlene about how this was nothing compared to what she'd been through. I had no idea what that meant, and I didn't want to know. In fact, I wanted to wash my hands of London Everly. A cab pulled up to the curb and I climbed inside.

"Where to, buddy?" the driver asked.

I sat there for a moment and didn't answer him.

"Hey, buddy? Are we gonna sit here all day?"

Fuck.

"Stay right here. I'll be right back," I firmly spoke.

I climbed out of the cab, walked back inside London's apartment building, and grabbed her suitcase.

"Come on, let's go," I said as I walked away.

"Wait. What are you doing? Where are we going?"

"Back to my place. You're going to stay with me until you find another Airbnb."

"No, Damien. You don't have to do that."

"I know I don't. But you did do me a favor last night and this is the least I can do. Just get in the cab, London."

I threw her large suitcase in the trunk and climbed in next to her.

"829 Park Avenue," I spoke to the cab driver.

"You didn't even ask me if I wanted to stay at your place," she spoke. "You just grabbed my suitcase and walked away like the rude person you are. I know you're not doing this out of the goodness of your heart because, to be honest, I'm not really sure there's a lot of good in you."

"Oh snap." The cab driver laughed.

I narrowed my eye at her.

"Don't look at me like that, Mr. Prescott."

"Again, who the hell do you think you are talking to me that way?"

"A woman who doesn't drop to her knees when you snap your fingers." She arched her brow.

"Wow. Did you really just say that?"

"I did and I'll say it again if I have to. I just don't understand why you can't leave me alone. It's obvious you don't like me, and trust me, I'm fine with that because I don't like you very much either."

"Is that so?" I asked.

"Yeah. It is so."

"I'm giving you a place to temporarily stay so you don't have to sleep in some cheap fuck of a hotel in an unsafe city and you're being very ungrateful."

"Oh, so now you think you're my knight in shining armor, rescuing the poor damsel in distress?"

"I'm nobody's knight in shining armor, London, and I never will be." I turned and looked out the window. "I'm done arguing with you. You're staying at my place and you're going to appreciate what I'm doing for you."

The cab driver pulled up to my building. I slid my credit card through and handed him a nice cash tip.

"This is for having to listen to all of that," I spoke.

"Thanks, buddy. You two are like a freaking soap opera." He laughed.

I sighed as I climbed out of the cab and took London's suitcase from the trunk. As we walked into the building, she felt the need to stop and talk to Sammy, the doorman.

"Hi, I'm London." She extended her hand.

"Hello, London. I'm Sammy."

"It's nice to meet you, Sammy. I'm going to be staying with Mr. Prescott for a couple of days, so I thought I'd introduce myself."

"My, aren't you a breath of fresh air." He grinned. "The pleasure is all mine."

"London, come on," I spoke with irritation as the elevator doors opened.

CHAPTER NINE

*L*ondon

He inserted a key into the slot labeled "PH12" and the elevator began to go up.

"You're at the top?" I asked.

"Yes. Is that a problem?"

"No. I bet the view is amazing."

"It's okay."

The door opened and I was greeted by an elegant marbled floor and an oval curved staircase in a dark mahogany. His place was beautifully decorated with mahogany wood floors and walls that were coated in a light gray color.

"You can take the guest bedroom upstairs. It's the only bedroom up there. Follow me," he spoke.

I followed him up a few stairs where there was a landing and to the right was a bedroom.

"What's up there?" I pointed to the rest of the stairs.

"It's the solarium room. There's a TV up there, a sectional, and a bar. Feel free to use it. In fact, you can just have this whole upper part of the house. That way, we won't be in each other's way."

We entered the bedroom and Damien set my suitcase in the

corner. The room was stunning with its gray painted walls and a queen size bed with a white down comforter. There was a beautiful white dresser with matching night stands on each side of the bed, and a large TV that hung on the wall above a white fireplace that sat directly across from the bed.

"This is beautiful. Did you decorate it?"

"No. I had an interior designer."

"I figured as much." I yawned and rubbed the back of my neck.

"Are you feeling okay? You look a little pale."

"I'm fine. Just tired. It's been quite a day."

"Then take a nap."

"I think I will," I said as I sat down on the bed.

"Okay. Help yourself to the kitchen later if you get hungry. The refrigerator is stocked."

"Thanks."

He walked out of the room and shut the door. The moment my head hit the oversized pillow, I was out.

ஓ

Damien

I went downstairs and poured myself a bourbon. I couldn't believe I'd asked her to stay here. I was not a fan of having houseguests, but as long as she stayed upstairs, we'd be fine. Plus, it was only for a couple nights until she found an Airbnb. As I downed the last of my drink, my phone rang.

"Damien Prescott."

"Damien, It's Don Bradbury."

"Hi, Don. How are you?"

"I'm good. Listen, I've given our dinner last night a lot of thought and I've decided to sign with your company."

My heart started racing as I made a fist and a wide smile crossed my face.

"Thank you, Don. You won't regret it."

"You and your future fiancée were very impressive. Of course your company and ideas were too. I see a bright future for the both of you, Damien."

I rolled my eyes.

"Thank you, Don. She is the love of my life." I could barely speak the words.

We said our goodbyes and I immediately called Scott.

"What's up, Damien?"

"I just got off the phone with Bradbury. We got the account."

"Yes!" he exclaimed. "I knew we would."

"How about we meet up and celebrate?"

"I'd love to, man, but Madison and I are taking her parents out to dinner for their anniversary."

"No problem. We'll celebrate another time. Have a good dinner."

"Thanks, Damien. I'll talk to you later."

I ended the call, poured another bourbon, and went into the media room to shoot some pool before I sat down to do some work. Before I knew it, a couple hours had passed.

"I see you do, do something other than work 24/7." London smirked as she stood in the entranceway to the media room.

I glanced up at her before shooting the eight ball into the left corner pocket.

"Is there something you needed?"

"I just came down to grab a bottle of water if that's okay."

"Sure. I told you the refrigerator is stocked," I spoke.

"Thanks." She smiled.

I sighed as I watched her walk away. I set down my pool stick and followed her into the kitchen.

"Did your nap help?"

"It did." She nodded.

"I got a call from Bradbury. We got the account."

"That's great." She grinned. "Congratulations."

"Thanks. He really liked you. So, thanks again for helping me out."

"You're welcome." She smiled as she walked by and placed her hand on my cheek. "I hope you can sleep at night knowing you lied to him," she spoke as she walked out of the kitchen.

"Excuse me?" I loudly voiced as I followed her up the stairs.

"What?" She laughed. "You did lie and you can't deny it."

"I'm not denying anything. Getting that account is a huge deal for my company and if I had to tell a little white lie to get it, so be it. No harm done," I said as I followed her into the bedroom.

"And what are you going to tell him when I'm out of your life in a couple of days?"

"He's going back to Seattle, so he won't know. And if sometime down the road he asks, I'll just tell him things didn't work out like we planned."

"Okay." She glanced up at me as she put her shoes on.

"Are you going somewhere?" I asked.

"Yes."

She got up from the bed, grabbed her purse and a blanket, and walked out of the room.

"Where are you going?"

"Central Park."

"It's going to be dark soon."

"And?" she asked as she walked down the stairs.

"And it's not safe. You're not from here, so you don't know. Plus, you don't know your way around Central Park."

"I'll figure it out."

She climbed into the elevator and gave me a small wave and smile as the doors shut.

I closed my eyes for a moment, clenched my fist, and inhaled a sharp breath.

"Dammit," I shouted with fury as I picked up the penthouse phone. "Sammy, do not let London leave this building. Do you understand me?"

"No, sir. I'm not sure I do."

"She's on her way down. Keep her inside the building until I get down there."

"Yes, sir."

CHAPTER TEN

*L*ondon
        The moment I stepped off the elevator, Sammy walked over to me.

"It's lovely to see you again, London." He smiled.

"Hi, Sammy."

"So, may I ask where you're off to?"

"Central Park." I smiled.

"Very nice. If you'll come over here with me for a moment, I'd be happy to give you the map to Central Park and I can point out which areas I think you'd really enjoy."

"How sweet of you." I placed my hand on his shoulder. "I'd love that."

I followed him over to the corner by the door and he pulled out a map of Central Park and opened it up.

"You are not going to Central Park by yourself at this time of the evening," Damien spoke as he walked up behind me.

"I'm sorry, and you are who to tell me what I can and can't do?" I asked as I turned around and stared into his eyes.

"The person you're staying with for a couple of nights and apparently now your damn babysitter."

"Just because I'm staying in your guestroom doesn't mean you can tell me what to do. I'm twenty-five years old. I don't need a babysitter. I travel alone, Mr. Prescott."

"I don't care. You're a beautiful young woman and you're not going to Central Park by yourself tonight."

"Then are you coming with me?" I asked as I placed my hands on my hips.

"I guess I don't have a choice."

"Don't you have work to do?" I cocked my head.

"Yes. I have a lot of work to do and you're taking me away from it."

I glanced over at Sammy and gave him a smile.

"Thank you, Sammy, and I'm sorry you have to hear all this."

"No worries, London. Have fun in Central Park."

"I won't be if he's tagging along." I turned and walked out the door.

"You think you're so funny." He followed behind me down the street. "Where the hell are you going? Central Park is the other way."

"I'm stopping at this little Thai restaurant on the corner that I saw. I'm hungry."

"For fuck sakes. Are you serious?"

"Go home, Mr. Prescott." I put my hand up.

"You do not tell me what to do. Understand me?" he firmly spoke.

I rolled my eyes as I stepped inside the restaurant and walked up to the counter.

"Hello. May I help you?" the kind man behind the counter asked.

I looked up at the menu that was hanging on the wall.

"I would like the Chicken Pad Thai and an order of your spring rolls, please."

"For here or to go?" he asked.

"To go. Mr. Prescott," I turned and looked at him, "would you like anything?"

He let out a sigh and placed his order.

"I'll have the drunken noodles with shrimp. Medium spice."

He rang up our order and gave me the total. I reached in my purse and grabbed my wallet.

"I got it," Damien spoke with irritation.

"No, no. Let me pay. It's the least I can do for your amazing hospitality." I smirked.

"I said I got it." His eye narrowed at me as he handed the nice man his credit card. "Add two bottles of water onto that."

"Your order will be up in about fifteen minutes. You may have a seat over there." He pointed to the long red couch that sat against the wall by the door.

Damien and I sat down and waited for our food.

"Thank you for dinner," I spoke.

"You're welcome," he replied as he stared straight ahead. "I'm going to ask you to stop doing something because it's really getting on my last nerve."

"What?" I asked.

"For the love of god, stop calling me Mr. Prescott. It's Damien. Got it?"

"Okay. Got it." I smiled as I nudged his shoulder with mine.

He slowly turned his head and narrowed his eye at me.

"Don't do that," he spoke.

"Your order is ready," the man behind the counter spoke as he held up a bag.

We both got up and Damien took the bag from him and we walked out the door.

"Aren't we going to take a cab?" I asked.

"No. The East entrance to the park is only a five-minute walk from here."

"Okay." I grinned.

"Why did you decide tonight to go to Central Park? You have a month to see it."

"Because it's a beautiful night and I just wanted to go and sit somewhere peaceful and enjoy a nice dinner."

"You call Thai carry-out a nice dinner?" He glanced over at me.

"Yeah. I do. Are you going to be okay?" I asked.

"What are you talking about?"

"You're not working."

"And who do I have to thank for that?"

"I didn't ask you to come. I was perfectly fine going by myself."

"That's just dumb, London. During the day it's fine, but at night, no. Think about it for a second. You sitting all alone on a blanket eating Thai food. You're the perfect target for some deranged person, and trust me, the city is full of them."

"I can take care of myself, Damien."

"Maybe you can or maybe you can't, but I'm not taking the chance. That's not something I want to carry around the rest of my life."

"Aw, so you do like me." I nudged his shoulder.

"I told you not to do that, and whether I like you or not is still up in the air. Right now, I'm not liking you very much."

I rolled my eyes as we entered the park.

"Follow me. I think there's something you might like to see," he said.

I followed him a short distance until we reached a large bronze statue.

"Is that the famous Alice In Wonderland statue?" I asked with excitement.

"Yes. You've heard of it?"

"Of course!" I ran up to it. "This is one of the reasons why I wanted to see Central Park. Oh my gosh, look at it. It's beautiful. Alice In Wonderland was my favorite Disney movie when I was a kid."

I set the blanket down and pulled my phone from my purse.

"Can you take a picture of me?" I asked as I handed him my phone.

I sat down on the mushroom in front of Alice and smiled. He took the picture and handed me my phone.

"Good job, Damien," I spoke as I looked at the picture.

"We better eat now while there's still a little bit of light left. Once it gets dark, we're going to have to leave this area."

We took a seat on the benches across from the statue, pulled our cartons of food from the bag, and began eating.

"Since you're staying as a guest in my penthouse, I want your story," Damien said. "You flew directly from Nashville to New York. Where were you before Nashville?"

"Chicago."

"Do you not have a job?" he asked.

"I do some freelance work, as you know."

"Some freelance work doesn't pay for all these little adventures you're going on. How the hell do you afford it? Are you living off credit cards or something?"

"I have one credit card and I have a savings account. I did have a job at a marketing firm, and when my mom passed away three years ago, she left me with a sizeable life insurance settlement."

"I'm sorry about your mom. Am I to assume there's no father in the picture?"

"I never knew my father. In fact, he doesn't even know I exist. My mother had a falling out with her parents when she was nineteen years old. She packed a bag and went to London to visit a friend of hers who was attending college there. She met a man and fell in love. Little did she know he was married and had two children. She found out he was married right before she discovered she was pregnant. So she broke it off with him and moved back to the States. It was just me and her since I was a baby."

"So he never knew about you?" he asked.

"Nope."

"May I ask how she passed away?"

"Stage four lymphoma. She died within six months after she was diagnosed."

"I'm sorry."

"Thank you. I appreciate it." I softly smiled at him.

"You collected life insurance money and quit your job to travel the world? What are you running from?" His brow arched.

"I'm not running from anything. My mother was forty-two years old when she died. You never know when your time is up and I want to make sure I see and do the things I've always wanted to before my time expires."

"You're twenty-five years old. You have plenty of time. What are you going to do when your money runs out? Have you even thought about that?"

"I'll figure it out."

"You're either a brave woman or a stupid one. I haven't decided yet," he spoke.

"There's more to life than money, Damien."

"Money is what makes a life, London. I grew up in poverty and I'm never going back there again."

"And there's a fine line between work and appreciating life."

"I appreciate my life. I appreciate all the hard work I put into my company and the millions of dollars I make."

CHAPTER ELEVEN

*D*amien

This beautiful girl was very irresponsible. Quitting her job to travel the world on the little money she had was stupid. She wasn't even thinking about her future, and once her little adventures were over, she'd have nothing.

"Like I said before, Damien, there's more to life than just making loads of money," she softly spoke.

"Having money makes me happy, and as long as I can make a shitload of it, I'm going to."

"Okay." She placed her hand on my leg. "You do that, but money doesn't buy happiness."

"I'm done talking about this," I spoke as I got up from the bench. "We better head back. It's getting really dark and I have work to do. You can come back during the day, by yourself."

"I will." She grinned.

The thing that irritated me about her was that she was always smiling and happy. It was annoying because she wasn't living in reality.

"You better start looking for an Airbnb when we get back to the penthouse," I firmly spoke.

"I will. Don't worry. I'll be out of your hair soon enough."

When we stepped into the lobby of my building, I froze when I saw Katherine standing there.

"Katherine, what are you doing here?" I asked in a stern voice.

"I left some of my jewelry in your bedroom and I want it back. Who's this?" she asked as she pointed to London.

"I'm London Everly." She extended her hand with a smile and I knew this wasn't going to go well.

"Oh, so you were fucking her too?" Katherine asked in anger as she dismissed London's hand.

"No, Katherine." I pushed the button to the elevator and the doors opened.

"You're a liar, Damien!"

The moment we stepped off the elevator, Katherine stormed down the hall and into my bedroom.

"Girlfriend?" London asked.

"No. She was never my girlfriend." I sighed as I went to the bedroom to make sure she didn't steal anything of mine.

"You're a real scumbag, Damien Prescott." Katherine pointed at me.

"Get your jewelry and leave," I spoke. "And don't ever come back here again."

"You don't have to worry about that."

She grabbed her jewelry and stormed out of the bedroom.

"You can have him," she spat at London. "But just beware, he's a liar, a cheater, and the most uncaring, emotionally unavailable man I've ever met in my life. He's toxic. So do yourself a favor and run as fast as you can before he breaks your heart." She stepped into the elevator, and before the doors closed, she looked at London.

"Don't say I didn't warn you."

"She sure is angry. What did you do to her?" London asked me as she followed me into my study.

"I did nothing to her. She's just pissed off because she thought we were in a relationship and I had to set her straight."

"You didn't love her?"

"God no. She was just a friend I fucked and took to dinner a couple times a week. She was more trouble than what it was all worth. I have work to do. You better get upstairs and start looking for another place."

"Okay. Good night, Damien."

I didn't respond and took a seat behind my desk. After working for a couple of hours, I turned off the light in my study and walked out. As I was on my way to the media room to shoot some pool before going to bed, I stopped at the staircase and looked up, wondering if London was sleeping or not. Why did I care?

I tossed and turned all night because of her. She was in my head and I couldn't get her out. I kept thinking about Central Park and how excited and happy she was when she saw the Alice In Wonderland statue. I thought about the conversation we had. I just thought about her. *Fuck.*

The next morning, I got up, showered, and noticed a smell infiltrating the penthouse. Was she cooking? I walked into the kitchen and found her at the stove in nothing but her pink, slightly sheer nightshirt.

"What are you doing?" I asked.

"Hey, good morning." She turned around with a smile across her face. "I'm making pancakes."

I walked over to the Nespresso machine and made a cup of coffee.

"None for me. I have to get to the office."

"It's Sunday," she spoke.

"I'm well aware of what day it is. Just because it's Sunday doesn't mean I don't work."

"Here's the deal. I won't say a word about you working on Sunday as long as you eat some breakfast first. If you don't like pancakes, I can make you something else."

I stared at her with a narrowed eye for a moment and then grabbed my coffee cup.

"Fine. I'll have pancakes. I haven't had those in years."

"Great." She smiled and turned back to the stove. "They'll be ready in a minute."

I took a seat at the island and stared at her long, lean legs and the outline of her perfectly shaped ass through her nightshirt. My cock was starting to twitch and I needed to divert my mind to something else.

"Where did you get the stuff to make the pancakes?" I asked.

"I had everything delivered and Sammy was kind enough to bring the bags up for me."

"I sure hope you were wearing something over that nightshirt."

"I had my robe on, but then I got too hot."

She placed three neatly stacked pancakes on a plate then walked over to the refrigerator, grabbed a can of whipped cream, and drew a smiley face on the top pancake and placed the plate in front of me.

"Seriously?" I looked at her.

"A smile first thing in the morning sets your tone for the day." She grinned. "You should try it some time."

I clenched my jaw as I picked up the bottle of syrup and poured it over the pancakes.

"Did you find an Airbnb yet?" I asked.

"I found a couple nice ones last night. I sent out emails, but I haven't heard back yet."

"Hopefully, you hear back today," I spoke.

"I'm sure I will."

"I hate to say this, but these pancakes are delicious."

"Thanks, Damien." She smiled. "Did it hurt you to say that?"

"A little." I smiled.

"Look at that. You know you're a lot sexier when you smile." Her grin grew wider.

"Don't get too used to it," I spoke.

She laughed as she turned around and placed her plate in the dishwasher. As she was cleaning the pan in the sink, I got up and placed my plate on the counter next to her.

"Excuse me," she spoke.

"What?"

"You are more than capable of placing your plate in the dishwasher." She started to laugh.

"What is so funny?"

She grabbed the kitchen towel and brought it up to my forehead. Instantly, I grabbed her wrist.

"You have a glob of whipped cream on your forehead. How did you manage that?" She continued to laugh as she wiped it off.

"I have no clue." I laughed with her as I removed my hand from her wrist.

Her laugh halted as we stared into each other's eyes.

"I like your laugh, Mr. Prescott."

I brought my hand up to her cheek as I stared at her beautiful mouth. Slowly, we both leaned in and our lips met for the first time. She dropped the towel and placed her arms around my neck as our soft kiss deepened.

"I'm sorry." I pulled back. "I shouldn't have done that."

"Don't apologize. I wanted you to," she whispered.

"Are you sure?"

"Yes. I'm more than sure."

Our lips met once again and my hands traveled up her nightshirt and cupped her ass, giving it a gentle squeeze. A soft moan erupted from her as her hands tangled through my hair. I placed my arms under her legs, picked her up, and carried her to my bedroom. Setting her in front of the bed, I gripped the edge of her nightshirt and pulled it over her head. My fingers traced the outline of her perfectly shaped breasts as her nipples hardened at my touch.

CHAPTER TWELVE

*L*ondon

My skin trembled beneath his fingers, which softly stroked me. His tongue glided across my neck as I felt the warmth of his breath near my ear. My fingers deftly unbuttoned his shirt and slid it off his shoulders, revealing his well-defined biceps and six-pack he sported underneath. I gasped when his hand traveled down the front of my panties. It had been a long time since a man made me feel this way.

"Lie down," he spoke.

I did as he asked while he took down his pants, revealing his large, rock hard cock. I smiled as I looked into his eyes while he gripped the sides of my panties and pulled them off. Immediately, his tongue traveled up my inner thigh until it reached my wet opening. A moan escaped him as his mouth explored my most sensitive area. His hands reached up and took hold of my breasts as he fondled them, taking my hardened peaks between his fingers. His tongue circled around me as he dipped his finger inside, sending my body into overdrive and on the brink of an orgasm.

"I want you to come for me. I'm not stopping until you do," he spoke.

I could feel myself swelling and exhilaration tore through me as an orgasm erupted. I let out several moans as he continued pleasuring me. My heart was racing as his tongue traveled up my torso, circling every inch of my skin until he made his way up to my breasts and then finally placing his mouth on mine. He hovered over me, our lips locked together as I ran my fingers through his hair. He broke our kiss, reached over, and opened the drawer of the nightstand and pulled out a condom. After putting it on, he hovered over me and slowly pushed himself inside, inch by inch. Our lips meshed as he thrust in and out. My nails dug into the flesh of his back as we both moaned with pleasure.

He halted and rolled on his back, bringing me on top of him. I stared down at him, my hands planted firmly on his chest as I rode him. He placed his hands on my breasts as my body got ready to explode.

"You're going to come again. I can feel it inside you. Don't stop. I'm coming with you," he panted.

At the same time, we both let out a loud moan as we orgasmed together.

"Oh my god," he groaned as he placed his hands firmly on my hips.

I leaned down and wrapped my arms around his neck, my breath erratic as my heart pounded out of my chest. His arms tightened around me as we both lay there waiting for our hearts to slow down. I rolled off him and he removed the condom and set it on the nightstand.

"I like your bedroom." I smiled.

"Thanks." He chuckled. "I really need to get to the office. What are your plans for today?"

"I'm going to spend the day in Central Park. It looks like a beautiful day out."

"Okay," he said as he got up from the bed and started putting his clothes back on.

I climbed off the bed and slipped into my nightshirt.

"Have a good day at the office. Try not to work too hard." I grinned as I placed my hand on his chest and walked out of his room.

I went up to my bedroom and sat on the edge of the bed. Sex with

Damien was amazing and now I knew I needed to get the hell out of here as quickly as possible. I grabbed my phone from the nightstand and checked my email with the hopes that one of the Airbnb's I emailed last night had replied. Nothing. I sighed as I set my phone down.

I spent the day in Central Park, exploring and taking pictures with my camera. When I got back to the penthouse, I found Damien in the media room playing pool.

"Hey." I smiled.

"Hey. How was Central Park?"

"Wonderful. I took a bunch of pictures."

"That's good." He leaned over the pool table and took a shot.

"I'm just going to go upstairs."

"Do you play pool?" he asked.

"No. I've never played."

He walked over to where the sticks hung on a rack on the wall and took one out.

"If you want to try, I can teach you."

"Sure. Just let me go put my camera away. I'll be right back."

Exhaustion settled its way inside me as I climbed up the stairs. I set my camera on the dresser and went back down to the media room.

"Okay, hot shot. Show me what you've got." I smiled.

He held out a stick and I took it from his hand.

"Choose a ball first. Then place the tip of the cue behind it."

"Like this?" I asked as I glanced at him.

"Yes. But hold the stick close to your hip. Don't grip it too tight. Just grip it with a relaxed hand."

"You make this sound so dirty." I grinned.

His brow arched at me as a smirk crossed his lips.

"Now place your hand on the table and place the tip of the stick between your thumb and index finger."

"Like this?" I asked.

"Yes. Now lean forward and stare at the center of the ball."

He stood behind me and placed his hands on my hips, moving me slightly to the center. I took in a deep breath at his touch.

"Do you mind if I shoot with you just so you get the feel of it?" he asked.

"No. Not at all."

My heart began to rapidly speed as his body leaned against mine and he placed his hand where mine was.

"You good?" he whispered softly in my ear.

I turned my head and stared into his eyes.

"I think so," I spoke as I stared at his lips, which were mere inches from mine.

"Are you sure?" He inched closer as his mouth met mine.

My hand let go of the pool stick and I turned around in his arms as our soft kiss turned into a passionate one. He lifted me up and sat me on the edge of the pool table and my legs wrapped around his waist. His mouth trailed across my neck as my hands tangled in his hair. I was breathless and getting wetter with every stroke of his tongue. He gripped the bottom of my shirt and pulled it over my head as our lips seduced each other's. My fingers fumbled with the buttons on his shirt and I slid it off his shoulders. He lifted me off the pool table and took down my pants and then set me back on it. My skin became heated as the anticipation of having sex on the pool table excited me. Damien pulled a condom from his wallet and slid it over his hard cock.

"Lie down and spread your legs for me," he commanded.

I did as he asked, my back pressed against the felt. His hand traveled up my inner thigh until his finger dipped inside me. I gasped and stared into his eyes. His other hand made its way up to my breast as he took turns fondling each one while his fingers explored me.

"You are incredibly beautiful, London. Seeing you like this has me so damn hard, it hurts."

A moan escaped me as he bent down and his tongue started circling around my sensitive area that was about to explode. The things he could do with his tongue were pure art and sent my body into oblivion. I panted and moaned as an orgasm tore through me.

"Beautiful." He smiled as he looked at me.

He smashed his mouth against mine before taking hold of my hand and helping me up. He scooted me to the edge of the table and thrust himself inside me, letting out a sexy moan as he swiftly moved in and out.

"Lean back," he said.

Placing my hands on the table, I leaned back, closed my eyes for a moment, and took in every bit of pleasure he gave me.

"Fuck yes. Oh my god, you're so beautiful and you feel so good. "Come with me."

Several moans escaped me as he picked up the pace and his grip on my hips tightened.

"Don't stop," I groaned.

"You don't have to worry about that," he panted.

Another orgasm overtook me as I yelled out in ecstasy. He halted and moaned as he buried himself deep inside me and exploded.

CHAPTER THIRTEEN

*D*amien

I stood there, buried inside her as I tried to regain my breath. It was the second time today that I fucked her and both times were exceptional. While I was at the office, I couldn't stop thinking about our morning romp and my cock craved her even more. I pulled out of her, took her hand, and helped her off the pool table. Shit. I had never had sex on this pool table. I never wanted to with any woman, but with her, it was all I envisioned. I removed the condom and threw it in the trash. She looked exhausted, so I picked her up and carried her to my bedroom, laying her gently on the bed. I climbed in next to her and she snuggled against me; her head laid on my chest.

"I'm so tired," she softly spoke.

"Go to sleep." I kissed the top of her head.

As soon as she was asleep, I climbed out of bed, threw on a pair of sweatpants and a shirt, and headed to my bar for a glass of bourbon. My intercom went off and when I walked over and pressed the button, I saw Scott standing there.

"Bro, can I come up?"

"Of course. I'm in the media room."

As soon as I walked back, I heard the elevator ding and Scott stepped into the media room holding a black duffle bag.

"Again?" I cocked my head.

"Yep. We got into this huge fight and she kicked me out for the night and told me to stay with you."

I couldn't help but laugh.

"What was it about this time?"

"I don't even really know. I was sitting on the couch watching the game and she was talking to me and I just kept agreeing with everything she said. Before I knew it, she accused me of putting the game before her and she kicked me out. She told me not to come back until I appreciated her." He rolled his eyes.

"Well, you can stay here, but there's something you need to know first."

"What?"

"London is staying here."

"Excuse me?" He arched his brow. "How did that happen?"

"Long story short. I went to her apartment yesterday because I didn't like her attitude with me over text and a pipe burst in the wall and there was about two inches of water covering the place. She was going to go to a hotel, so I told her she could stay with me for a couple of nights until she found a new Airbnb to stay at."

"Seriously?" His brows furrowed. "You don't do shit like that."

"I stood her up yesterday at the Empire State Building and she did do me that favor for Bradbury, so I thought I could at least let her stay in one of the guestrooms to repay the favor."

"Damn, Damien. I can honestly say that I'm really shocked right now. That was—that was really nice of you."

"Stop." I put my hand up. "It's only for a couple of nights."

"Where is she now?"

"Asleep in my bed."

"Excuse me?" His brow arched again.

"We had sex this morning and again just a little bit ago."

"You're fucking her now?"

"I am a man and she is a beautiful woman. I have needs and she was here and willing."

A sly smile crossed his face and I knew damn well what he was thinking.

"No!" I pointed at him. "I am not. It's just sex."

"Okay. If you say so. I need a drink, man. Double bourbon on the rocks."

We sat up and talked until about midnight and then he went into one of the other guestrooms and I went to bed. When I walked into the bedroom, London opened her eyes.

"Oh my god, what time is it?"

"It's midnight," I spoke as I climbed in next to her.

"Shit. I slept that long?"

"Obviously, you needed it," I said.

She began to get out of bed and I stopped her by grabbing hold of her hand.

"Where are you going?"

"Back to my room."

"You can stay here. You don't have to go back to your room."

"Are you sure?" she asked.

"Yes. It's late."

She snuggled against me and laid her head on my chest. I nearly lost my breath.

"By the way, Scott is here. He's staying the night."

"Why?" She lifted her head and looked at me.

"Madison kicked him out again. It happens at least every three months. They get into a fight and she makes him come here."

London let out a light laugh.

"Then I shall make you both pancakes tomorrow morning." She grinned.

"Sounds good. But make sure you're dressed and not in your night-shirt when he's around."

"Deal." She laid her head back on my chest.

*T*he next morning, my alarm buzzed, and after I shut it off, I rolled over and stared at the empty space where London lay all night. Getting up, I showered and got ready for work, and when I walked into the kitchen, I found her and Scott laughing.

"Good morning." London smiled.

"Morning." I walked over to the coffee machine and made a cup of coffee.

"Damien, look. She made a smiley face on my pancakes. My mom used to do that for me when I was a kid," Scott spoke with excitement.

I took a seat at the island next to Scott and London set a plate of pancakes down in front of me.

"The two Airbnb's I inquired about emailed me back this morning. The one is no longer available, but the other one is."

"And where is that one located?" I asked.

"Harlem."

"Hell no. You can forget it. You are not staying in Harlem."

"Damien's right, London. You don't want to stay there, especially by yourself."

"I appreciate both of your concerns, but I can take care of myself."

"You are not staying there. End of discussion," I spoke in a firm voice.

"It's the only place I found that I can afford."

"Gee, I wonder why?" I cocked my head at her. "If there's nothing else, then you'll just have to stay here until you leave on your next adventure."

Scott quickly turned his head and looked at me with a shocked expression on his face.

"You really want me to stay here?" she asked.

"Why not? It's free. Save the money you'd spend on an Airbnb and use it for wherever you're off to next."

"I don't think that's a good idea. I'll keep looking."

"Why, when you can have all this? We seem to be getting along just fine. There's no reason for you to leave right now."

"I don't know, Damien. I think it's best I leave."

I finished off my pancakes and looked at her as I got up and took my plate to the sink.

"You're staying put. End of discussion. You're safe here and that's the way it's going to stay. I have to get to the office. Come on, Scott."

He followed me to the elevator and the moment we stepped inside and the doors shut, he smacked my arm.

"I knew it. You are falling for her."

"No I'm not. The city can be a cruel place and she has a place to stay without worry and I can have sex every day if I want it."

"Jesus Christ, Damien. Just admit it. Come on. I'm your friend and your partner. When Katherine told you she was going to Italy by herself, you told her to have a great time. You wouldn't even go with her."

"London is different," I spoke as we walked out of the elevator.

"Yeah. She's different alright. You have feelings for her and you don't want her to leave. But I got news for you, buddy, she's leaving in a month regardless of what you say. Staying in New York isn't her plan."

"I know. At least I'll get a month's worth of sex out of the deal." I smirked.

CHAPTER FOURTEEN

*L*ondon

While I was cleaning up the kitchen, a sickness rose inside me. He wanted me to stay here with him for the rest of my time in New York. Maybe it wasn't such a bad idea because then maybe I could convince him to do something other than work 24/7. If I could make him see that there was more to life than just work, I would feel I accomplished so much more than just seeing everything I wanted to here.

I grabbed a bottle of water, took it up to my room, and pulled open the drawer to the nightstand where my bottles of pills lay. I closed my eyes for a moment as a throbbing headache started to emerge.

"No. Not today, Teaghan. I wanted to go out and see things," I spoke to myself. "Damn you!"

I took my pills and lay down on the bed. Maybe I'd just rest for a while and then work on my blog and update all my followers on what I'd been doing while in New York.

When I awoke, I looked at my phone and it was two o'clock. Shit. I'd been asleep for six hours. I also noticed I had six text messages from Damien. I heard the elevator ding, so I climbed out of bed and stood at the top of the stairs.

"Why the fuck can't you respond to my text messages?" Damien asked in anger as he stepped off the elevator.

"I just saw them. I was taking a nap."

"Since nine o'clock this morning?"

"Yeah. I had a headache. I didn't plan on sleeping that long."

"Is your headache better?" he asked in a calmer voice.

"Yes." I smiled. "Why are you here and not at work?"

"Because you didn't respond to my text messages. I thought maybe you disobeyed my orders and moved to Harlem."

"Disobeyed your orders?" I laughed. "You cannot and will not order me around."

"Okay, maybe I worded that wrong."

"To put your mind at ease, I've decided to take you up on your offer and stay here until my time in New York is up."

"Good. You're a smart girl."

"On one condition."

"What is your condition?" He sighed.

"You take me to see the sights of New York."

"I can't do that, London. I have a job and a lot of work to do. I run a company. A company I built from the bottom up. I'm not taking time away from that to show you around the damn city."

"Okay." I shrugged. "Then I guess I'm moving to Harlem."

"The hell you are." He pointed his finger at me.

"Damien Prescott," I spoke as I slowly walked down the stairs and stood in front of him. "This is the last time I'm going to say this." I pressed my finger into his chest. "You do not get to tell me what I can and cannot do. You are not my keeper. You are not my husband. You are not even my boyfriend. You have no claim on me whatsoever. Understand?" I spoke in a firm voice.

His jaw clenched and anger filled his eyes.

"I've been traveling alone for months. I've been on my own since my mother passed away, and I don't answer to anyone. Got it? You came all the way home to yell at me for not answering your text messages. You're here and you don't need to go back to the office. I want to go to the Metropolitan Museum of Art and I would like you to come with me," I spoke in a stern voice, my finger still pressed into his chest.

"Fine," he spoke with anger. "You want to go to the damn museum, then let's go!"

"Thank you. I just need to change. I'll be right back." I smiled.

§

Damien

The nerve of that woman. Who the hell did she think she was? I pulled my phone from my pocket and dialed Joslyn.

"Hello, Mr. Prescott," she answered.

"Joslyn, I won't be coming back to the office today. Reschedule my four o'clock meeting with the staff."

"What? You're not coming back? Are you feeling okay?"

"I'm feeling fine. I have something I need to take care of," I spoke in a stern voice.

"Okay. See you tomorrow morning," she said.

I ended the call, and within seconds, my phone rang and it was Scott.

"What?" I answered.

"Joslyn just said you aren't coming back and you cancelled the staff meeting. What the hell is going on?"

"I'm taking London to the art museum."

"What?" He laughed.

"Just be quiet. Did you talk to Madison?"

"Yeah. She told me I could come home tonight. I'll swing by and pick up my things."

"Okay. Just let yourself up in case I'm not home."

"Will do, Damien. Have fun." He chuckled.

"I'm ready." London smiled as she walked down the stairs.

"Just for the record, I'm working the second we get back here."

"That's fine."

We exited the lobby of my building and I hailed a cab for us. When we climbed inside, the cab driver was the same one who drove us the other day from her Airbnb to my penthouse.

"Hello there," He smiled. You two again."

"Hi." London smiled back.

"Metropolitan Museum of Art," I spoke in an irritated tone.

"Don't mind him. He's just mad because I'm taking him away from his work."

"He was mad last time he was in my cab," the driver said.

"He's always in a constant state of madness. And you want to know why?"

"Why?"

"Because he works too much."

"You," I pointed to the driver, "concentrate on the road, and you," I pointed to London, "be quiet."

She leaned over and kissed my cheek.

"You're going to be okay, Damien."

I sighed as I shook my head and looked out the window. The driver pulled up to the museum and I slid my credit card through and handed him a cash tip.

"Thank you." London smiled at him as she climbed out.

"You're welcome. Have a good time."

"May I ask why you wanted to come here so bad?" I asked.

"I love art. When I was a kid, I used to read all about Renaissance artists. Plus, this the largest art museum in the United States."

I purchased our tickets and our journey began. I watched her as she looked around at the architecture of the building. Her eyes danced with delight as a smile never left her lips. Being here made her happy. We walked around and looked at all the various art. I'd been here a thousand times, so none of it was new to me. But to her, it was, and I could tell she was taking every bit of it in.

She stopped in front of the first painting she saw by Claude Monet and stared at it intently.

"Everyone discusses my art and pretends to understand as if it were necessary to understand, when it is simply necessary to love," she spoke.

"Huh?" I glanced over at her.

"That was a quote by Claude Monet. He's saying we don't need to understand what he paints, we just need to find the beauty in what we're seeing. Kind of like people. Sometimes we don't need to understand them or try to understand them. We just need to love them."

"Oh," I spoke. "Did you know he tried to kill himself because of financial difficulties? See, money was important to him too."

She rolled her eyes at me and walked away.

"What? It's true."

They announced over the speaker that the museum would be closing in fifteen minutes.

"We better wrap this up. They're getting ready to close. Plus, I'm starving, so we need to go grab some dinner."

I took hold of her hand, the first time since we'd been out, and led her out of the museum.

"What are you in the mood for?" I asked.

"Pizza." She grinned.

"Okay. We'll go to Serafina's, then."

CHAPTER FIFTEEN

*L*ondon
    After eating an amazing pizza and salad, we went back to Damien's penthouse. The thing I noticed was when we were at the museum, he seemed a little more relaxed and his anger about having to miss work seemed to have dissipated slightly.

"I'm going into my study to work. What are you going to do?" he asked.

"I think I'm going to take a bath."

"Use my master bathroom. You'll like it a lot better."

"I will. Thanks." I smiled.

I uploaded all the pictures I'd taken since I arrived in New York onto my laptop. I opened up my blog and began writing about my experience here so far. I was flooded with messages from people asking me where I'd been the past few days.

"London?" Damien opened the door.

I shut my laptop and set it beside me on the bed.

"Hi."

"I thought you were going to take a bath?"

"I am, right now. I just wanted to get the pictures I'd taken uploaded on my laptop."

"It's been an hour."

"I know." I got up from the bed. "I had to go through each one and see if they needed editing. Why are you checking up on me?"

"I don't know. I was thinking about maybe joining you." He smirked.

"Really?" I grinned. The two of us taking a bath together?"

"It's just a thought. If you don't want to."

"I didn't say that, Mr. Prescott." I smiled as I grabbed his shirt and led him downstairs.

We stepped into the bathroom and Damien started the water.

"I'll be right back," I said as I left the bathroom, ran up the stairs, and grabbed a rose-scented bubble stick I bought from Lush.

"What is that?" he asked as I held it under the stream of water.

"A bubble stick from Lush. It's amazing. You'll love it. I hope you like the scent of roses."

"Really, London?"

"Yes. Trust me." I smiled.

He climbed in first and lay back. After stripping out of my clothes, I climbed in and snuggled my body against his. I could instantly feel his cock getting hard and pressing against me.

"Really, Damien?"

"What? Like I can help it. I just watched you strip out of your clothes, your body is amazing, and now you're lying against me in a bubble-filled tub naked. I am a man, after all."

I let out a laugh as I lay in his arms and thought about how nice this was.

"Can I ask you a question?"

"Sure. What is it?"

"You're what? Around thirty-ish?"

"I'm thirty years old. Why?"

"How is it that you own such a successful advertising business worth millions at your age?"

"I started selling my advertising services when I was fifteen years old. Like I told you before, I came from poverty. My mother was a drug addict and my father was an alcoholic. They spent whatever money they made on drugs and alcohol. I had nothing. I slept on a mattress on the floor and wore shoes that were too small. I spent my days after school in the library and on the computer, just so I didn't have to go home. One day, I ran across this ad for a bike shop and it was the worst ad I'd ever seen. So I played around and created a new ad, emailed it to the company, and told them that I thought this was a way better concept for them. They loved it and asked me if I could do more. I did and they paid me. I thought if I could do that for them, I wondered what other companies would like my ideas, so I started searching and found a couple more. I saved every single dime, and when I was sixteen, I left home and never looked back."

"Where did you go?"

"I came here. I'm originally from New Jersey. I rented a room from a nice old lady who needed the extra cash and enrolled in high school so I could finish and get my diploma. That was where I met Scott. He had the same visions as me. We started traveling from company to company pitching ideas. Some loved us, some didn't. Their loss. It wasn't easy, but we kept at it. We both made our first million by the time we were nineteen years old. We invested, took some college classes about business and finance, and when we turned twenty-one, we opened the doors to the Prescott Group. So now do you understand why I work as hard as I do? Why work is my life?"

"I do understand and I'm sorry about your parents and how they treated you." I lifted my head and looked at him. "You're letting fear control your life."

"What do you mean?"

"Your fear is not having money and that reminds you of your childhood. It's the driving force that is consuming your life with work. You need to slow down, Damien, and appreciate what you have now. Appreciate the people around you. The gifts the world has to offer. You need to live every day as if it's your last. You can't let the beauty of life pass you by because you're so consumed with your work and the fear that if you don't work, you're going to lose everything. You've built a magnificent company, you're already set. But what is life if it only revolves around work?"

He stared into my eyes and took in every word I spoke. Or at least I hoped he did.

"Are you sure you're only twenty-five?" He smirked. "Because you seem wise beyond your years. I'm not like you, London. I'm going to be honest with you. I think what you're doing is crazy and irresponsible. I'm sorry and I don't mean to hurt you, but I think you're running from your own fears."

"I'm not running from anything. I don't have any fears. I'm living my life the way I want to."

"Okay, then. You live your life and I'll live mine." He brought his hand up to my cheek. "Don't be mad at me."

"I'm not." I reached up and kissed his lips.

After we got out of the bath, we climbed into his bed and made love. I still had time with him and I was going to use it wisely.

"Where are you going to next?" he asked as I lay wrapped up in his arms.

"I think I'll go to the Grand Canyon. My dream is to go to Paris and see the Eiffel Tower in person, sip French coffee in a cute little Parisian café, and eat pastries until I get sick. But I'm not sure that is going to happen."

"Why? Because you can't afford it?"

"Something like that." I smiled.

"Well, maybe you can get a job and save and then you can go to Paris."

"Yeah. Maybe I should do that."

CHAPTER SIXTEEN

One Week Later

*D*amien
       I was sitting behind my desk, staring out the window, when Scott walked into my office.

"You look like you're in deep thought, my friend."

I turned my chair around and placed my hands behind my head as I leaned back.

"I was just thinking about London and how she's leaving in two weeks."

"That sucks. I really like her."

"Yeah. Me too."

"Gee, really? I never would have guessed." He smirked. "Get her to stay."

"She won't. She dead set on these damn life adventures."

"Where is she going to next?"

"She says the Grand Canyon."

"Then take her there yourself. Spend a week and bring her back. In fact, tell her you'll take her wherever she wants to go as long as she agrees to come back with you. Do you love her, Damien?"

"I don't know." I sighed. "And I can't just be hopping on planes going to random places. I have a company to run."

"It's not going to kill you to take a week here and there off. I'm here and the company will be here when you get back."

"I can't."

"By the way, what are you doing tonight?" he asked.

"Probably having dinner with London. Why?"

"Umm. She and Madison are going out to a club tonight. You didn't know that?"

"No. She didn't say a word about it," I spoke with irritation.

"Oh. Well, maybe she was going to tell you today. Since they're going out, why don't we head to a bar or something?"

"Which club are they going to?"

"Madison said something about a club called NightHawk. I guess it just opened a couple of months ago."

"Then that's where we're going," I spoke.

"Damien. That's not a good idea."

"Really?" I arched my brow at him. "You think it's safe for those two beautiful young women to be going to a club alone?"

"Madison will kill me if I told her I was coming. They're having a girls' night out. No men allowed."

"I didn't even know they talked," I said.

"Apparently, they do. I didn't know either."

"We'll go and make sure they don't see us. That place is going to be packed with people."

"I don't know, man." He slowly shook his head.

"What's the matter? Are you afraid of your wife?" My brow raised.

"No. Of course not. Not really."

"Good. Then we're going. We'll figure out a time later."

"Okay." He sighed as he got up from his chair. "Plan on having another houseguest if they see us."

He walked out of my office and I immediately picked up my phone and called London.

"Hello," she answered.

"Hey there, beautiful. How about dinner at Tavern on the Green tonight? I can make a reservation."

"I'd love that, but I'm going out with Madison tonight."

"You are?"

"Yeah. How about tomorrow night?"

"Where are the two of you going?"

"She wants to check out this new club that opened up a couple months ago called NightHawk."

"Oh. You really want to go there instead of having dinner with me?"

"I have dinner with you every night, Damien, and I will have dinner with you tomorrow night. Tonight is a girls' night. It's been a long time since I've had one of those. You understand, right?"

"Yeah. Of course I do. What time are you two leaving?"

"We're leaving here around seven thirty."

"Okay. Then I'll see you before you leave. I'll be home around six o'clock."

"Sounds good. See you later."

After ending the call, I walked down to Scott's office.

"They're leaving the penthouse at seven thirty. Meet me outside my building at seven forty-five."

"Okay." He sighed.

❧

I arrived home at six fifteen and called out London's name.

"I'm in my bedroom," she shouted.

I walked up the stairs and into the room, where I found her standing there looking in the closet wrapped in nothing but a towel.

"Hi." She smiled. "How was your day?"

"Shit." I walked over from behind, wrapped my arms around her, and began softly stroking her neck with my tongue. "I know something you can give me that will make it a whole lot better," I whispered.

"Is that so?" She brought her hand up to the back of my head.

"Yes." I lightly nipped her earlobe.

She turned around in my arms and softly kissed my lips while her fingers undid my belt. I quickly took off my shirt and let out a light moan as I removed the towel from her and firmly gripped her breasts. She successfully took down my pants and underwear, releasing my throbbing cock, which was already hard and ready for her. She got down on her knees, grabbed my cock with her hand, and wrapped her lips around the tip of it. I almost came right then and there. I wasn't expecting that, but I wasn't about to stop her. Her mouth hugged my shaft as her head moved up and down, giving me long, smooth strokes. I threw my head back in pleasure as I placed my hands on each side of her head, tangling my fingers through her soft, silky hair. Her tongue rolled around me as she gently squeezed my balls with her hand. Fuck. This was the best blowjob I'd ever had. My knees grew weak with each sensual stroke her mouth gave me.

"That's enough, baby. I need to bury my cock inside you right now."

I guided her up as her tongue licked its way up my body until our lips met. Picking her up, I placed her on the bed and told her to get down on her knees. I wanted to take her from behind for I knew how much she loved it.

"I'm not using a condom this time. I won't come in you," I spoke as I stood at the edge of the bed, grabbed her hips, and thrust deep inside her. She gasped as did I when I felt the warmth of her envelope my cock. I reached one hand around her and played with her clit as I thrust in and out of her at a rapid pace. My breath was heavy and her moans grew louder with every stroke. She orgasmed and her come coated my cock even more. A couple more strokes and the buildup was there. I was about to explode, so I pulled out and shot myself all over her beautiful bare back.

"Oh my god," I spoke with bated breath.

I stood there, unable to move for a moment. She turned her head and looked at me with a smile on her face.

"All better now?"

"Definitely." I grinned back at her.

I went into the bathroom, grabbed some tissues, and cleaned her up. She rolled on her back and I couldn't help but grab her arms and hold them over her head as I hovered over her.

"Thank you." I tenderly kissed her lips.

"You're welcome."

Staring into her eyes, I felt nothing but pain. Pain at the thought that I would never see her again. This was too much. I'd never let myself fall for anyone. Hell, that wasn't true at all. No woman had ever made me feel what I felt for her and agony rose inside me.

CHAPTER SEVENTEEN

Damien

She put on the same black dress that she wore the night she went with me to my business dinner with Bradbury. Which, as far as I was concerned, was way too sexy to go to a club in. The guys there were going to salivate, and their dicks would be hard all night staring at her. I didn't dare say anything about it because she'd give me attitude. I wasn't worried because I was going to be there to keep an eye on things.

"Hey, Madison." I kissed her cheek. "You look stunning."

"Thank you, Damien. Scott told me the two of you are going out."

"Yeah. We're just going to grab some dinner and then come back here and play some pool."

"You are?" London asked. "You didn't mention that."

"It was a last-minute thing. Plus, we have some work things to discuss over dinner."

"Oh." She smiled. "Okay. Have fun. Don't wait up for me." She placed her hand on my chest.

"You're not going to be that late, are you?"

"Why, Damien? Does she have a curfew or something? She's your houseguest, not your wife." Madison gave me the evil eye.

"No, Madison. She doesn't have a curfew. I just want the two of you to be careful. Things get sketchy in the city after a certain time."

"Don't worry, big guy. She's in good hands with me." Madison smirked.

I waited until seven forty and walked down to the lobby of my building and waited for Scott to arrive.

"Good evening, Mr. Prescott." Sammy smiled.

"Good evening, Sammy."

"I saw London leaving. How much longer will she be staying with you?"

"She's leaving town in less than two weeks."

"Ah. She told me she was going to see the Grand Canyon. It's going to be sad not seeing her perky smile and bright face around here every day."

"Yeah. It will be." I placed my hand on his shoulder.

"Maybe you could convince her to stay?"

"I'm thinking about it." I smiled.

"Don't take this the wrong way, Mr. Prescott, but London seems to bring out the best in you. There's something to be said for that."

"Thanks, Sammy. I'm starting to see that she does. Scott just pulled up. I'll see you later."

I climbed into the cab and Scott looked at me.

"You know, we can always just go to dinner," he said.

"Or we can go and make sure our girls stay safe."

"Did you just hear yourself? You called London your girl."

I looked at him and smiled.

We had the driver park across the street so we could see the people who were in line before heading in. Madison and London weren't standing in it, which meant they were already inside. I paid the driver and Scott and I crossed the street and walked up to the bouncer who stood there with his arms folded and a grizzly look on his face.

"Hey, buddy. Long time no see." I turned my hand over and showed him the folded hundred-dollar bill.

"Nice to see you again." He firmly shook my hand and took the money. "Go right in."

"Thank you." I smiled.

The club was packed with wall to wall people as we looked around to try and find the girls.

"There they are." Scott pointed to the dance floor.

I pulled out my wallet and another hundred-dollar bill and walked up to a table that sat in the corner.

"Hello, ladies. This hundred is yours if you let me and my friend here have your table."

"Sure." The redhead beamed with excitement as she grabbed it out of my hand and she and her friend walked away.

"I need a drink," Scott said. "Do you want a bourbon?" he asked me.

"Sure."

He went to the bar and I sat there and watched the two of them dance. I had the perfect view as long as they stayed right where they were. A couple guys approached them and I instantly stood up. They left and I sat back down. Scott finally returned with our drinks and took the seat next to me. We both sat there and watched them dance the night away, then they took a seat at an empty table by the dance floor. London guzzled a glass of water. The thought just occurred to me that since I'd known her, she had never once had a drink of alcohol.

"Hey, handsome, may my friend and I join you for a drink?" a woman with long black hair who looked like a hooker asked.

"No. You may not. Move along."

"Whatever, asshole," she spoke as she shot me a disgusted look.

I looked back over to where London and Madison were sitting, and all of a sudden, London fell out of her chair and onto the floor.

"What the fuck!" I shouted as I got up from my seat and Scott and I ran over to the table. "What happened?" I asked Madison as I bent down next to London.

"I don't know. We were just talking, and all of a sudden, she started slurring her words and fell off the chair."

"Call 911 now! She's having a seizure," I yelled at Scott. "London." I rolled her on her side as her body was clenched tightly and shook. "You're going to be okay."

Her seizure stopped and I gently rolled her on her back as I placed my hand on her forehead. Her eyes were wide as she stared at me.

"An ambulance is on its way," I spoke.

"No. No hospital," she spoke in a panicked tone.

The paramedics arrived and placed her on a stretcher. I climbed in the back of the ambulance and held her hand.

"Have you ever had a seizure before?"

"Not in a long time," she whispered as she turned her head and looked away from me.

We arrived at the emergency room and I followed the paramedics until I was stopped by a nurse.

"Excuse me, sir? Are you her husband?"

"No. I'm not."

"Are you a blood relative?"

"No."

"Then you need to stay out here." She put her hand up in front of me.

CHAPTER EIGHTEEN

*L*ondon

"Do you want me to go get the man who came in with you?" the doctor asked.

"No. I just want to go home."

"Okay. I'll get you discharged," he somberly spoke as he placed his hand on mine.

The nurse wheeled me out to the waiting room where Damien sat.

"Jesus Christ. They wouldn't let me see you. Are you okay? What did the doctor say?"

"Not much. I just need to go home and rest."

"I'm going to grab a cab. I'll be right back," he spoke.

A moment later, Damien walked over, wheeled me out the doors of the emergency room, and helped me into a cab.

"There has to be a reason why you had that seizure, London. You've had them before. You said you hadn't had one in a long time."

"Damien, I'm sorry, but I am just so tired and out of it." I laid my head on his shoulder.

He didn't say another word, and when the cab pulled up to his building, he picked me up and carried me to the elevator, into the penthouse and to his bedroom, setting me on the bed. He undressed me, slipped my nightshirt over my head, and pulled the covers back.

"What were you doing at the club?" I asked.

"We can talk about that tomorrow. Just get some sleep." He kissed my forehead and walked out of the room.

Damien

$\mathcal{I}$ walked over to the bar and poured myself a drink. I wanted fucking answers. What if I wouldn't have been there? And what did she mean by "not much"? There had to be a reason why she had a seizure. What the hell wasn't she telling me?

I heard her quietly walk up the stairs, so I waited until she was in the bedroom and I went up. When I pushed open the door, I found her hunched over the nightstand with the drawer open. The moment she heard me, she quickly shut it.

"What are you doing?" I asked.

"Looking for something," she nervously replied.

"Looking for what?"

"You know what? It doesn't matter. I can look tomorrow. Let's go to bed." She smiled as she walked over to me and took hold of my hand.

I pulled my hand away and walked over to the nightstand.

"Damien, don't."

I opened the drawer to see an array of prescription pill bottles lying there. My heart started rapidly pounding.

"What is this, London?" I asked without turning around and looking at her.

"Just some pills I take."

"Just some pills?" I shouted in anger.

"Damien, stop right now."

"Don't you dare tell me to stop!" I shouted as I turned around and faced her. "What is all this? Are you a fucking drug addict? Are you addicted to pills? Is that why you had the seizure? Because I know,

London. I know what a pill addict is. I grew up with one! My God, is this the reason you're always sleeping?" I grabbed the pills one by one and threw them on the bed. "Did you take one too many before you went out tonight?" I threw another bottle down. "You didn't want me in that hospital room with you tonight, did you? You were scared I was going to find out about your little problem."

"Stop it!" She grabbed the sides of her head.

"Don't you dare tell me to stop it! This is my home! You said you hadn't had a seizure in a very long time? What happened? Were you a drug addict and then got clean and slipped up again? Did something happen back in Minnesota and that's why you ran away, quit your job, and decided to spend whatever money you got from your mother's life insurance to travel around the US? Did you get into some trouble?" I shouted. "I want you out of my house!" I pointed at her.

She stood there and stared at me as tears fell from her eyes.

"Okay. I'll pack my things and go."

"Damn right you will. Fuck this and fuck you," I spoke as I stormed out of the bedroom.

CHAPTER NINETEEN

L ondon
    I never meant for him to find out. The less he knew, the better off we both were. I understood his anger. He felt betrayed, just like he did by his parents. I grabbed my suitcase with my trembling hands and neatly packed my things. I was exhausted and my head was pounding, but I was strong, just not strong enough to walk away without an explanation. I loved him. It wasn't part of the plan and I tried so hard to keep my emotions out of it, but I couldn't. He was unlike anyone I'd ever met before. I didn't want his pity, but right now he hated me and maybe it was for the best. It would be easier this way. I had thought a lot about the day I'd walk out of here and go to my next destination, and every single time, it brought tears to my eyes. I found myself loving it here and loving him, but I couldn't stay and he would have to understand that. I inhaled a deep breath, composed myself, and went downstairs, where I found him sitting on the couch in the media room with a drink in his hand.

"Just fucking go, London. I don't ever want to see you again."

"I'm so sorry, Damien. None of this was supposed to happen. I never should have agreed to stay here."

"Damn right you shouldn't have, and I never should have offered." He downed his drink. "Just go. Get out of my fucking life."

I had to weigh the options as to what would cause him more pain: him believing I was a drug addict or the truth. I needed just to go and put all this behind me. I'd catch a plane to Arizona first thing tomorrow morning.

"I hope you can forgive me." I turned and walked away.

"London!" he shouted. "It's the middle of the fucking night. Just go to bed. I want you out of here by time I get home tomorrow."

"Thank you, Damien."

He got up from the couch and walked over to where I was standing.

"Don't you ever fucking say those words to me again," he spoke through gritted teeth, walked away, and slammed his bedroom door shut.

I climbed into bed and held the covers tightly against me. He'd be okay over time.

&❧

Damien

I slept an hour at the most. My head was filled with anger and my heart was filled with pain. This was what I got for letting someone into my life. Never fucking again. I'd learned my lesson. I got up, got dressed, and prayed she wasn't up yet. Hell, maybe she already left. Good riddance. I got to the office and I was in the worst mood ever.

"Joslyn, get me a fucking cup of coffee now!" I shouted.

"Yes, sir." She quickly got up from her chair.

"What the hell is the matter with you?" Scott asked as he followed me into my office. "How is London? I was texting you all night and you never answered. Madison was texting London and she didn't answer."

"I kicked her out."

"What the fuck, man?"

"She's a drug addict. I found a bunch of pills in her nightstand drawer."

Joslyn walked in and set my coffee down on my desk.

"Did she try to deny it?" Scott asked.

"Nope. When I told her to get the hell out of my house, she just said okay and that she'd go. No explanation, nothing. I can't believe how fucking stupid I am. I knew something was up with the way she was always tired and sleeping all the time."

"Excuse me, Mr. Prescott?" Joslyn spoke.

"Can't you see I'm in the middle of a conversation? What do you want?" I shouted.

"There's something you should know."

"Jesus Christ, Joslyn. What is it?" I sighed.

"London isn't a drug addict. She's dying."

"What?" I laughed. "Is that what she told you? Because drug addicts are really good liars."

"She didn't tell me anything. I follow her blog. I've been following her journey for about a year. I knew she was coming to New York and I was going to contact her to see if she wanted to meet for coffee because I wanted to praise her on her strength. Then she walked in here with your wallet and I couldn't believe it. I couldn't bring myself to say anything to her because, I don't know, I felt weird and I didn't know quite what to say. If you'll hand me a piece of paper, I'll write down her blog address and you can check it out for yourself."

"Damien," Scott quietly spoke.

I sat there and swallowed the lump in my throat as I handed Joslyn a piece of paper and a pen.

"I'm not surprised she didn't tell you. She only stays in one place for a month or so to see everything she sets out to. Mr. Prescott, she's fulfilling her bucket list before she dies."

"Thank you for telling me, Joslyn," I softly spoke. "I'm sorry I yelled at you."

"It's okay. I'm used to it." She smiled slightly before walking out of my office.

"I can't believe this, Damien. My god, what did you do?"

"She could have told me last night, but she didn't. She was never going to tell me. She was going to leave in two weeks and I never would have known. Can you give me some time alone, please?"

"Yeah, sure, man." He placed his hand on my shoulder.

I stared at the piece of paper with her blog address for a moment. I turned to my computer, typed it in the address bar, and hit the return key. I started reading and scrolling. Pictures of her at the Empire State Building, Central Park, a Starbucks, and other places filled the screen. A video of her giving a tour of her Airbnb cut into me like nothing other. There were pictures of Tennessee, Chicago, and Florida. I scrolled further down, reading her posts about what she was doing, what she'd seen, how she felt. She had an inoperable brain tumor in an area of her brainstem that was much too dangerous and impossible to remove. She referred to her tumor as "Teaghan," and as I scrolled down farther, I came across a letter she had written. Tears filled my eyes and the lump in my throat was bigger than ever as I sat and read it.

Dear Teaghan,

We first met when I was ten years old. You wanted to be friends and I accepted you at first. But I was the one in control and you didn't like that, so you took it upon yourself to make me very sick. Sick to the point where it was time to end our friendship and say goodbye. But after the surgery, a part of you was still there, inside me, lying dormant and plotting your return. I get it. I really do. You were pissed. I'd be too if someone cut ninety-five percent of me away. I said goodbye to our friendship, and I thought you accepted it. Now, all these years later, you decided to rekindle what we had and come back bigger and stronger. You nestled yourself away into the depths of my brain where you knew nobody could touch you. If you think you've won, you haven't. The fact is we're all going to die at some point in our lives. For some, it's unexpected and out of the clear blue. But you've given me the courtesy of giving me time to do every-thing I want to do and see before my time is up and you completely take over me. You may have taken things from me such as marriage and starting a family, but that is all. I've accepted you into my life again and I'm going to live each remaining day to the fullest, seeing and doing everything I'd always dreamed of, and that is something you can't take away from me. Til the end, my dear friend.
- London

I wiped my eyes and leaned back in my chair, trying to catch my breath. What the fuck had I done? I pushed the intercom button on the phone and asked Joslyn to come into my office immediately.

"Yes, Mr. Prescott?"

"Cancel all of my meetings for today. To be honest, cancel them for the rest of the week. I don't know when I'll be back." I got up from my chair and put my suitcoat on.

"Where are you going?"

"To find London and do what's right."

"Oh, Mr. Prescott. I'm so happy to hear that." She clapped.

I hailed a cab back to my penthouse and looked around for Sammy in the lobby, but he wasn't there. The minute I stepped into the penthouse, I ran up the stairs and into her bedroom. Her suitcase was gone.

"Shit!"

I looked at my watch. It was ten o'clock. I pulled my phone out and dialed Joslyn.

"Joslyn, get online right now with the airlines and see what time the flights to Arizona are leaving."

"How do you know which airline she's flying with?"

"Shit. Well, she flew Delta from Tennessee to New York. With any luck, she'll fly that again. Hurry up and call me back. I'm going to pack."

I ran down to my room, grabbed my suitcase, and started throwing clothes in it. Once I finished, I took the elevator down to the lobby and saw Sammy.

"Sammy!" I ran up to him. "What time did London leave the building?"

"She left about an hour ago with her suitcase. She said she was going to Paris and hugged me goodbye."

"Paris! She's supposed to be going to the Grand Canyon!"

I pulled out my phone and called Joslyn.

"Forget Arizona. What time is the flight to Paris? Sammy said she left an hour ago, so there's no way she got on a plane yet."

"I'm pulling it up now. If she left an hour ago, she must be on the 11:50 flight. She wouldn't have made the one before that."

"Book me two tickets in first class."

"Mr. Prescott, you're not going to make it in time."

"I'll make it. Book them now."

"There's two seats left, row two, seats C & D."

"Book them now. Put it on the company card. I'm on my way to the airport. Wait, they're not the Suite seats, are they?"

"No."

"Okay. Book them."

"And what if she's not on that flight?"

"Then we'll keep searching until we find which flight she's on. I don't care how much it fucking costs."

"I'm on it, Mr. Prescott."

"Thanks, Joslyn."

"Don't you need your passport, Mr. Prescott?" Sammy asked.

"Shit! Watch my luggage and get me a cab!"

I pushed the button to the elevator and thanked god that the doors opened immediately. I ran to my study, opened my safe, grabbed my passport, and took the elevator back down.

"Your luggage and your cab, sir." He smiled.

"Thanks, Sammy."

"Where to, buddy?" the driver asked.

"LaGuardia and step on it. I need to get there as soon as possible."

"I'll do my best."

I reached into my wallet and pulled out a hundred-dollar bill.

"You'll do your best?" I handed it to him.

"I will get you there ASAP." He smiled.

The cab driver pulled up to the curb and I grabbed my luggage and flew out of the cab and into the airport.

"ID and passport, please," the man behind the counter spoke.

I pulled out my passport, handed it to him, and then pulled my ID out of my wallet.

"You have two seats?" he asked in confusion.

"Umm. Yes. I don't like anyone sitting next to me on a long flight."

"Thank you very much, Mr. Prescott. Enjoy your flight." He smiled.

"Thanks."

The line for sky priority wasn't long at all and I couldn't believe it. Everything was moving quickly. Once I got through security and ran through the airport to my gate, they were already boarding. I placed my phone on the scanner and was cleared to go. I took in a deep breath as I stepped onto the plane, praying she was on this flight. Placing my bag on my seat, I stepped out of first class and let out a sigh of relief when I saw her sitting in a seat with her head leaning against the window, staring out. I headed towards her and stopped when our eyes met.

"Damien? What—How?"

"We need to talk, London." I held out my hand to her and the lady sitting next to her gave me a dirty look. "Excuse me, ma'am, but she needs to get out of her seat and come sit in first class with me."

"Damien, what are you doing? Did you buy a ticket?"

"I bought two first class tickets. I'm going with you to Paris." I smiled.

"How did you know I was on this flight?"

"I talked to Sammy and he said you told him you were going to Paris, so I had Joslyn look up the times and this is the time that made the most sense. Come on. Come with me."

"I can't believe you did this."

She placed her hand in mine as the woman sitting next to her got up from her seat, and I led her to first class.

"Take the window seat," I spoke.

"Thank you."

As soon as we both sat down and got settled, I grabbed hold of her hand.

"London, I'm so sorry for the things I said to you." I brought her hand up to my lips. "I will never be able to apologize enough to you."

"Damien, there's something—"

"I already know." I gave her hand a gentle squeeze.

"How?"

"Apparently, Joslyn is one of your followers. She told me about your blog. Wow. You have over five hundred thousand followers."

"I'm sorry." She looked down.

"Don't be. I don't want to talk about it right now. Not here. Not on the plane. I want to talk when we're alone and in private. For now, let's just enjoy each other's company."

"I can't believe you're coming to Paris with me." She smiled as tears filled her eyes.

"Believe it. We're going to have an amazing time."

"But what about work?"

"What about it? Scott is there and the company will be there when I get back. The only thing that matters is spending time with you in Paris." I brought my hand up to her cheek and softly kissed her lips. "Did you book a hotel yet? If you didn't, I'll book one."

"No. I was just going to kind of wing it when I got there."

"Well, I'm here now and there will be no winging it." I winked.

I pulled my phone from my pocket and googled Paris hotels. It was imperative that I found one with views of the Eiffel Tower from the room. I found the perfect hotel and booked us the perfect room.

"Done. Reservations are set for the Shangri La."

"Sounds fancy." She grinned.

CHAPTER TWENTY

*L*ondon
   I couldn't believe he was sitting next to me. He knew about the tumor, and yet, he still wanted to be with me. After our four-hour layover in Boston, we finally arrived in Paris the next morning at six a.m. and the not-so-smooth landing jolted both of us awake.

"Damn it," Damien spoke.

"No swearing. We're in Paris." I grinned as I stared out the window.

Damien took my hand and we exited the plane. When we got to baggage claim, I saw a man dressed in all black holding a sign with the name "Prescott" across it.

"Look, there's your name." I smiled.

"That must be our driver."

We grabbed our luggage, climbed into the car, and headed to the hotel. When we arrived, our room wasn't ready because, technically, check in wasn't until three p.m.

"Do you have any rooms at all available right now?" Damien asked.

"Yes. We have a few."

"Then give us your standard room and call me when ours is ready."

"Very well, sir."

When we entered our temporary room, Damien wrapped his arms around me and held me tight.

"Are you hungry?" he asked.

"Yeah. I am. But I need a shower first."

"Me too." He smiled.

"There's only one bathroom." I smirked.

"Then I guess we'll have to take one together." His lips softly pressed against mine.

After our incredibly long shower, my body still reeled with the pleasure he gave me. I didn't want to come down from the feeling of this fairytale I found myself in, but reality wasn't too far behind and I was prepared for it.

"Great news. The front desk called and our room is ready," Damien spoke.

"Already? I didn't expect it to be until this afternoon."

The bellhop knocked on the door, handed Damien our new room key, and took our luggage. When we stepped inside the elevator, it took us all the way to the top floor. The hotel was breathtaking, and I couldn't wait to see what our new room had to offer. The moment we stepped inside, the first thing I saw from the living area window was the Eiffel Tower. I ran to the large glass sliding doors that led out to a mammoth terrace, opened them, and stepped outside. The view was absolutely stunning.

"Beautiful, isn't it?" Damien asked as he wrapped his arms around me from behind.

"I've never seen anything so magnificent in my life," I softly spoke.

"Let's go find a café and sip on some French coffee and have some breakfast." He kissed my head.

"I'd love to. But first," I turned around in his arms, "I have to take my pills."

"I'll go get you a bottle of water." His lips pressed against my forehead.

I walked back into the room and took in the beauty of it all. From the French-styled furniture, marbled floors, and a touch of elegant Asian décor throughout, this suite was every girl's dream. After sipping

French coffee and eating breakfast in a quaint little Parisian café, Damien told me he had a surprise for me: a beautiful horse and carriage ride through Paris.

"When did you have time to arrange this?" I asked.

"I sent an email to the hotel when I booked the room. I figured what better way to see Paris." He smiled.

"You've never been here?"

"No. I was always too busy working." He lightly gripped my hand.

We climbed into the carriage and off we went.

"We'll come back tonight when it's dark and see the tower lit up," he spoke. "London, why didn't you tell me about your tumor? Why didn't you tell me that night?"

"Because the last thing I want is your pity. The symptoms are getting worse and the last thing I wanted was for you to get involved with Teaghan. This is my battle and my battle alone. I didn't expect to meet someone like you along my journey. It wasn't part of my plan and the last thing I wanted was to drag you into it. As you remember, I was only supposed to stay with you for a couple of nights and be on my way. But then we grew closer and it became really complicated."

"So you were just going to leave at the end of the month and never tell me?"

"Yes, because it was better that way."

"Not for me it wouldn't have been. I had plans, London. Plans to get you to stay in New York with me. I wanted to make you see that you could build a life there and that you didn't have to keep traveling from place to place. But I didn't know you were only doing those things because you were trying to fulfill your bucket list."

"I was ten years old when Teaghan first made her appearance. After numerous scans, the doctors felt she was isolated, so they decided to put me on some medication to try and shrink it. The doctor said that surgery was too risky at that point. So I went on the meds and they didn't work. I became sicker with each day that passed. Finally, the doctor decided it was time to go in and try to remove Teaghan. He was able to remove ninety-five percent of her. He couldn't get to the other five percent and he couldn't guarantee that she wouldn't grow back. So I underwent radiation for three months and back for scans every six months. She was stabilized and I was no longer experiencing any symptoms. Then it got to the point where I only needed to go back once a year. When I turned eighteen, I stopped going because I was healthy, and if she'd stayed dormant for eight years, I was in the clear. It wasn't until after my mother passed away that I started experiencing symptoms again, and I knew in my heart that she was back. I put off going to the doctor for as long as I could because I already knew what they would tell me. Two years ago, I landed in the ER because I had such a killer headache and I'd been vomiting for three days straight. I was dehydrated and very weak. That's when the doctors confirmed that she was indeed back and growing at a high-speed rate. The doctor told me that because the tumor was so deep down into the brainstem that it was inoperable, but he wanted me to see another doctor, a colleague of his at the Mayo Clinic for a second opinion. I went and he told me the same thing. There was nothing they could do. I wasn't ready to accept it, so I went to see a specialist at the Cleveland Clinic and at John Hopkins. Both doctors extended their sympathy to me and said that the only thing they could offer me was a little more time. They put me on a medication cocktail to try and slow the growth of the tumor, an anti-seizure medication, and a headache medication for my headaches. But they warned me that the meds were only a band-aid and they would eventually stop working within a years time. That's when I decided I needed to try and fulfill my bucket list before my time was up. Damien, I'm at peace with my life. I've fully accepted it."

"All that talk about life being too short and you never know when your time is up, you were in a way trying to tell me. Weren't you?"

"Yes. I was."

"How do you know the cancer hasn't spread?"

"Teaghan isn't cancerous."

"What?" He furrowed his brows.

"She never was. She's very rare. But because she had grown the opposite way, deeper into my brain, she became inoperable. Eventually, she'll get so big that she'll start shutting down my body. I won't be able to walk, talk, see, or breathe on my own. I'll lose all control of any function. That's why I signed a DNR for when it happens. When I was in the ER the other night, they did a scan and discovered that the medications have probably stopped working because of the size of the tumor. But I'm still taking them every day with hope and faith that I have some time left. That's why I came to Paris, because I decided I wasn't going to die without seeing it first. I wasn't going to let her take that away from me. That's why I started my blog, because I wanted to leave something behind for people to remember me."

He pulled me into him and held me tight. I'd never felt as much peace as I did in his arms.

"You're not going through this alone anymore. I'm staying with you and I don't care what you say. We're doing this together, London. I'll take you anywhere you want to go. Anywhere in the entire world. You name it and we'll be there, together. Because if you think I'm going to let you go now, you're crazy."

CHAPTER TWENTY-ONE

*D*amien
          I held her in my arms after we made love and her head
rested peacefully on my chest. This was our fourth night in Paris and
we'd done a lot. She was exhausted and I could see the change in her
more every day. As I was holding her, thinking about what to do, she
had a seizure in her sleep. Her eyes flew open and her body started to
jerk. I rolled her on her other side and wrapped my arms lightly around
her while I pressed my lips against her forehead. The seizure stopped
and she closed her eyes and went back to sleep. This was too much for
her and I needed to get her back to New York so she could rest.

The next morning, while she slept, I got up and opened the laptop
that was sitting on the desk. I started researching brainstem tumors
and the top neurosurgeons in the world. There had to be something or
someone that could help her. I wasn't about to sit back and do nothing
for the woman I had fallen so deeply in love with. She had helped me
in ways I never thought possible, and now, I was going to help her. I
was looking at different countries, ones that were more medically
advanced. There had to be a goddamn trial study somewhere in the
world for brainstem tumors. Everywhere I looked, I kept seeing the
same name over and over again: Dr. Jamieson Finn. I googled him and

came across numerous articles about his work and awards. He worked out of Cedars-Sinai in Los Angeles and consulted at Mount Sinai in New York. It wouldn't hurt to give him a call. I picked up my phone and dialed his office number.

"Dr. Finn's office, how can I help you?"

"Umm. Yes, I need to make an appointment to see Dr. Finn, please."

"His next available appointment is next month."

"I don't have a month. I need to get in to see him now."

"I'm sorry, sir, but Dr. Finn is completely booked."

I took in a deep breath to stop me from losing my shit.

"I understand that, but this is an emergency. My girlfriend doesn't have a month. It is imperative that we get in to see Dr. Finn immediately."

"Sir. I'm sorry, but there's nothing I can do. He can only take so many appointments because he has his other duties here at the hospital."

I hung up on her and threw my phone across the desk. There had to be a way to get in to see him. I tried searching for his personal number and came to a dead end. Then I ran across an article about his wife. It seemed she was a trauma surgeon at the same hospital. I dialed the emergency room and a woman named Jackie answered.

"Hello, I need to speak with Dr. Grace Finn, please."

"May I ask who's calling?"

"Damien Prescott out of New York."

"Let me see if I can find her. I'm going to put you on hold."

I waited for approximately ten minutes and then someone picked up.

"Hi, Mr. Prescott, this is Dr. Grace Finn. How can I help you?"

Thank god.

"Dr. Finn, I know this isn't appropriate, but I'm in desperate need of your help. I tried calling your husband to get an appointment with him, but the utterly rude woman said his first appointment isn't until next month. My girlfriend doesn't have a month."

"Okay, Mr. Prescott. Why don't you tell me what's wrong with your girlfriend?"

"She's been diagnosed with an inoperable brain tumor in her brain-stem. She's been to several neurosurgeons and they've all said the same thing. She's been taking medication to try and keep the tumor under control to buy her more time, but her symptoms now are getting worse. She had a seizure last night in her sleep. Please, Dr. Finn. I love this woman so much and I need to get your husband's opinion. From what I've read, he's the best neurosurgeon out there."

"He is the best, Mr. Prescott."

"Please. I'm begging you for your help. I am not ready to lose her."

"Okay. Are you in the Los Angeles area by any chance?"

"No. I'm from New York, but right now, we're in Paris. It was her last wish."

"I see. What is your girlfriend's name?"

"London Everly. She has a blog where she's documented her jour-ney. Let me give you the web address and you and your husband can check it out."

"What is it and what is your phone number?"

I rattled off the web address to her as well as my number.

"Thank you, Mr. Prescott. I'll talk to my husband and I'll be in touch. I promise."

"Thank you, Dr. Finn."

CHAPTER TWENTY-TWO

*J*amieson Finn

"You paged me?" I asked Grace as I walked down to the ER.

"I just got a call from a man named Damien Prescott out of New York. It seems he tried to make an appointment with you, but your secretary couldn't accommodate him."

"So he called you? That takes a lot of nerve."

"Not really. He's desperate, Jamieson. His girlfriend has an inoperable brain tumor in her brainstem and her symptoms are worsening. Apparently, she's been to several specialists and they won't touch it. So they put her on some medication to try and control it to buy her some more time. He said she has a blog and he asked if we could check it out."

I sighed as I looked at my watch.

"I have a craniotomy in fifteen minutes."

"Fifteen minutes should be enough time." She smiled.

"Fine. Let's go up to my office."

I pulled up a chair next to mine and typed in the web address in the address bar, pulling up London's blog.

"Oh my gosh, she's beautiful," Grace spoke. "Look at how happy and full of life she is. You'd never know this girl has a brain tumor."

"No, you wouldn't," I replied.

I scrolled down, reading her posts and looking at her pictures.

"Dr. Finn, your patient is prepped for his craniotomy," Linda spoke as she poked her head through the door.

"I'll be there as soon as I can. I'm in the middle of something."

"Oh my God, Jamieson. She wrote a letter to her tumor," Grace spoke.

We both sat there and read it, and when I glanced over at Grace, I saw tears streaming down her face.

"You have to see her," she spoke. "This isn't an option, Jamieson."

"I know," I spoke as I tried to swallow the lump in my throat. "Did Mr. Prescott give you his number?"

"Yes. It's right here." She handed me a piece of paper.

I picked up my phone and dialed the number.

"Hello."

"Mr. Prescott, this is Dr. Jamieson Finn."

"Dr. Finn. Thank you so much for calling me back."

"No problem. My wife and I just looked at London's blog. Grace mentioned you were in Paris."

"Yes. We are. But it's wearing her down and fast."

"She also mentioned she had a seizure in her sleep last night? Has she had any other seizures prior?"

"She had one the other night at a club. The doctor at the ER said he suspects her meds are no longer working."

"Can you get her here tomorrow? I'll be here at the hospital all day. I will warn you that I might be in surgery or something, so you may have to wait."

"That's fine. We can catch a flight out this afternoon."

"Okay. I'll see you both tomorrow. I will try to do whatever I can, but I can't make any promises."

"I understand, Dr. Finn. Thank you. Thank you so much."

"You're welcome. Have a safe flight."

"You're my hero." Grace smiled as she kissed my cheek.

"I don't know if this woman can be saved, Grace. She might be in for another disappointment and I hate doing that."

"I know. But you also love challenges. This may be your biggest one yet." She smiled.

CHAPTER TWENTY-THREE

*D*amien
        I ended the call and let out a sigh of relief. Maybe, just maybe, there would be something Dr. Finn could do to help her. Now all I had to do was tell her, and I wasn't so sure how that was going to go.

"Did I hear you talking to someone?" London asked as she walked into the living area.

"Good morning." I smiled as I held out my arms and she took a seat in my lap. "Do you remember what happened last night?"

"What do you mean?"

"You had a seizure in your sleep, London."

"Shit." She laid her head on my shoulder.

"Listen to me. I'm taking you to Cedars-Sinai in Los Angeles to see Dr. Jamieson Finn. He's a world-renowned neurosurgeon and he's won many awards and accolades for his work. He said he'll see us tomorrow, so I'll book us a flight out to Los Angeles this afternoon."

She lifted her head from my shoulder and stared into my eyes.

"No, Damien."

"What do you mean, no? He might be able to help you, London."

She got up from my lap and walked into the bedroom.

"Don't walk away from me." I followed her.

"He can't help me. You need to let go of the notion that I can be fixed. I've been there, done that, and I'm not going through it again. Every time I walked into those damn doctor's offices, I had a tiny piece of hope inside me that the next one would say they could help me. But it was always the same answer. I've accepted my fate, Damien, and now you need to as well."

"The fuck I will!" I shouted. "There is a possibility he can help you. You need to explore all options. Dr. Finn is an option."

"And the possibility is greater that he can't!" she shouted back. "I'm not going through that disappointment again! I'm not walking in there for him to say what they've all said, 'I'm sorry, London, but the tumor is inoperable. There's no way we can get to it without killing you.'"

"You don't know that," I calmly spoke.

She walked over to me and placed her hand on my cheek.

"I do know that, Damien. I love you for trying, but there's no hope left. I'm sorry." She turned away and started heading towards the bathroom.

"You love me?!" I shouted in anger and she stopped. "If you truly loved me, you would do this for me and for you."

"This isn't about you. This is about me."

"You're wrong!" I yelled. "This is about me now. About trying to help the woman I fell madly in love with! I love you, London Everly, and I'm not ready to let you go! I fucking love you too much."

"Damien, stop," she spoke as she turned around and looked at me.

"No, I'm not going to stop." I walked over to where she stood. "I love you, London. I love you, and I'm not going to stop loving you. Teaghan can't take that away. She can't take away my love for you. You are the only woman I have ever loved my entire life. You are the woman who came into my life and made me see the beauty of it. You made me realize that there is more to life than just work and money. You did that!" Tears started streaming down my face as I gripped her hips and dropped to my knees, placing my head on her legs. "You breathed life into me. For the first time in my life, I feel like I'm living. Don't take that away from me. Give Dr. Finn a chance. Please."

She knelt down and wrapped her arms around me.

"It's okay. I'll go see Dr. Finn. We'll go see him." She tightened her grip around me.

❦

London

The moment we stepped onto the plane and took our seats, Damien grabbed my hand and brought it up to his lips.

"I love you." He smiled.

"I love you too." I laid my head on his shoulder.

He had called Scott and Joslyn and told them that we were on our way to Los Angeles and he didn't know when he'd be back in the office. California was on my bucket list. I had planned on going there after the Grand Canyon if time allowed it. I wasn't scared to go see Dr. Finn, because I already knew the outcome. I was scared for Damien because the little bit of hope he had would be destroyed. His breakdown killed me. I never in a million years would have thought he would have done something like that. He loved me, and as happy as I was that he did, I also felt his love for me would destroy him in the end, and I needed to make sure that didn't happen. I needed for him to see that his life would still go on and that he would find happiness again if he allowed it.

I opened up my laptop and uploaded the remaining pictures of Paris and a couple of me and Damien. I wanted the world to see that no matter what I was facing, this man loved me and wanted to face it with me. I recorded a video on the plane instead of writing a post. I wanted everyone to know that I was on my way to Los Angeles to see Dr. Finn for hopefully a miracle. I turned the camera on Damien and had him say hi. He gave a smile, waved, and then kissed my cheek. I was tired, so I ended the video, uploaded it, closed my laptop, and fell asleep on Damien's shoulder.

❦

*W*e arrived in Los Angeles the next day around noon. Instead of having a car pick us up, Damien rented a car.

"Do you know where we're staying?" I asked.

"No. We can figure that out after we see Dr. Finn."

"Oh," my brow arched, "so we're winging it?"

"We're winging it." He smirked.

We drove to Cedars-Sinai, and as we were looking for Dr. Finn's office, a woman in scrubs with a stethoscope around her neck stopped us.

"Oh my gosh, you're London." She smiled.

"Yes. Yes, I am."

"I'm Dr. Grace Finn. Dr. Finn's wife. We spoke on the phone, Mr. Prescott."

"Yes. Of course. Thank you so much." He lightly shook her hand.

Dr. Finn turned to me and gave me a hug.

"It's nice to meet you. I saw your blog. Your journey is amazing."

"Thank you." I smiled.

"Have you seen Jamieson yet?"

"No. We just flew in. We were looking for his office," Damien replied.

"Oh. You're in luck. I'm just on my way up there now. Follow me."

We followed her into the elevator and up to his office. She lightly knocked on the door before opening it.

"Jamieson, Mr. Prescott and London are here."

"Excellent. Come on in," he spoke as he got up from his desk and shook my hand and then Damien's. "Have a seat." Dr. Finn gestured to the chairs across from his desk.

He took his seat behind his desk and Grace stood next to him.

"So, London, I was able to get your medical records from when you were ten years old and had the tumor first removed. I see they only took out ninety-five percent of it and then you underwent radiation."

"Yes. That's correct."

"And now, it grew back. I have your medical records and scans from all the doctors you visited, but I haven't looked at any of them yet. I want to get a CT scan and an MRI and look at those first. I know you're a pro at those." He smiled.

"I am."

"Do you by chance have your medication on you?"

"I do." I reached into my purse and set the bag of pills on his desk.

"Great. I'll look these over while Grace takes you to the imaging room. I'll be there in few minutes. Damien, you can have a seat in the waiting room, and we'll come get you when she's done."

"Thank you, Dr. Finn," he spoke.

Damien turned to me and grabbed hold of both my hands.

"I love you, London. Good luck, baby."

"I love you too." I smiled as I kissed his lips.

CHAPTER TWENTY-FOUR

*J*amieson Finn
   I took a seat in the control room and Grace sat down next to me.

"How are you doing in there, London?" I asked through the intercom.

"I'm doing good, Dr. Finn." She gave me a thumbs-up.

Her scans started to slowly load on the computer screen.

"Well, hello there, Teaghan, you big, beautiful tumor," I said.

"Oh my god, Jamieson," Grace spoke as her pager went off. "Damn it. I gotta go, babe. There's a trauma coming in." She kissed my head.

I stared at the screen and intently studied the tumor. I saw why nobody would touch it. I sighed as I leaned back in my chair and continued to study the area surrounding the tumor. I looked at the machine and stared at London. This woman was so full of life despite this thing growing inside that was slowly killing her. Was this really impossible? It sort of looked that way and I had a decision to make, but then again, I didn't believe in the impossible.

"London, you're all done. Andrea will take you to get changed and then back to my office."

"Okay, Dr. Finn."

I stepped into the waiting room and told Damien to come back to my office with me. I saw the nervousness written all over him and I felt bad for the guy. As soon as we stepped inside, London walked in.

"You two can have a seat right here." I pointed to some chairs facing the monitors that were mounted on the wall.

Walking over to my computer, I pulled up London's new scans and placed the ones she had done over a year ago next to them.

"The tumor is starting to get bigger and out of control. But I'm going to say that this happened over the course of the past couple of months."

"Is the tumor operable, Dr. Finn?" Damien asked.

"I'm going to be very honest with you. I've only seen this type of tumor twice in my life, yours and my father's. Except my father's was malignant, and yours isn't, which actually makes it one I've never seen before. But, a tumor is a tumor as far as I'm concerned. I removed my father's, but yours is a little more complicated. There are significant, and I mean significant risks."

"Like what?" Damien asked.

"One wrong move or mistake and London will die on the table. She could suffer from respiratory disturbances and circulatory dysfunctions as well as many other deficits. She could lose her ability to talk, walk, even see. The risks are high, I'm not going to lie to you. I need a couple of days to think about this and then I'll be in touch. You are staying in Los Angeles, correct?"

"Yes. We're staying." London smiled.

"Dr. Finn, I don't understand," Damien spoke. "You can't tell us now whether you'll try to remove it or not?"

"No. There are things I need to work out first and study."

"If I don't have the surgery, how much longer do I have?" London asked.

"I'd say about a month before your body starts shutting down. Give me two days. It's all I'll need."

"Thank you, Dr. Finn," London spoke as she stood from her chair and shook my hand.

"Thank you." Damien shook my hand.

I left the hospital early, went home, had dinner with my family, and then went right into my study. I brought London's scans home with me along with the model of her brain and tumor. I sat at my desk and studied both.

"I made you a cup of coffee," Grace said as she set the cup down on my desk.

"Thanks, sweetheart."

"How's it looking?" she asked.

"Not good. The tumor is wrapped around this one vessel right here. There's no way I can get to it without damaging the vessel. What quality of life would she have if I did this surgery and something went wrong? She'd then wish she was dead. I don't know, Grace. I don't think I can do this. The risk is way too high. Higher than what it was for my father."

"Well, you need to make a decision either way." She kissed the top of my head and walked out.

As I was sipping my coffee and staring at the brain model, Ava, our seven-year-old daughter, walked in.

"Hi, Daddy. What are you doing?"

"I'm working, baby. Trying to see if I can save this woman's life."

She climbed on my lap and looked at the scans on my computer.

"That's a bad, bad tumor, Daddy."

"I know it is, baby, and I'm not sure there's anything I can do. See how part of the tumor is wrapped around this vessel. Daddy can't get to it without damaging the vessel."

She intently stared at it for a while.

"Sure you can, Daddy." She smiled as she looked at me.

"Is that so, little miss?" I arched my brow at her.

"Yes." She picked up the model brain and held it in her hands. "First, you'll go through underneath, right here." She pointed. "Remove part of the tumor from there, close her up, and then go through the top of the brain and remove the rest. Easy peasy." She grinned.

I looked at her and then took the model from her hands and held it up.

"It's not easy to go through there, sweetie."

"Sure it is, Daddy. You'll have to do it while she's sitting up."

I narrowed my eye at her and then looked at the model and then back at the scans.

"Oh my God, Ava." I kissed her head hard. "You're a genius."

"I know, Daddy." She giggled.

"Grace!" I shouted. "Grace!"

"What? What is it? What happened?" She ran into my study in a panic.

"I can do it. I can get to London's tumor that's wrapped around this vessel thanks to our genius daughter!"

"Huh?" She cocked her head.

"Tell her, baby. Tell Mommy what you told me." I handed her the brain model.

"Daddy can get to this part of the tumor by going through here first. Then when that part is removed, he can go into the top of the brain and remove rest. Easy peasy." She smiled.

"Pumpkin, that first area is impossible to get to because of the spinal cord," Grace spoke.

"Wait for it, Grace." I smiled.

"Not if Daddy does it while the patient is sitting up."

"Oh my God," Grace spoke. "Jamieson, she might be right. Do you think it'll work?"

"It'll work, Mommy."

CHAPTER TWENTY-FIVE

*L*ondon

Damien booked us a room at Casa Del Mar in Santa Monica right on the beach. The sun was about to set, so we went for a walk along the shoreline, hand in hand, and let the waves of the water wash over our feet. I was enjoying every second of this day I could and appreciating the beauty of it, because if by chance Dr. Finn decided to do the surgery, it might be the last time I'd see the sun set over the ocean water. As we were walking, Damien's phone rang.

"Hello? Hi, Dr. Finn. We're staying at Casa Del Mar in Santa Monica. Yes, of course. Just text me your address." He ended the call.

"What did he say?" I asked.

"He asked if we could come to his house. He was going to meet us somewhere, but he's only about ten minutes away."

"Did he say why?"

"No. I guess we'll find out when we get there. We should head to our room and go change."

I detected a nervousness in his voice, and I knew he was pained with worry, either that Dr. Finn would do the surgery or he wouldn't.

"Are you okay, baby?" He gently squeezed my hand as we drove to Dr. Finn's house.

"I'm fine, Damien. I've been through this before, multiple times. How are you?"

"I have a good feeling that he's going to give us good news. If he wasn't going to do the surgery, he wouldn't have asked us to come to his house tonight."

"Maybe," I spoke as I looked out the window.

We pulled up to Dr. Finn's house and Damien rang the doorbell. When the door opened, an adorable little girl with wavy long blonde hair answered.

"Hello, there," Damien spoke.

"Hi." I smiled as I bent down.

"Hi. I'm Ava. Are you the lady with brain tumor?" she asked.

"I am." I grinned.

"Come in."

"London, Damien, thanks for coming over," Jamieson spoke. "I see you met my daughter, Ava."

"She's adorable, Dr. Finn."

"Hey, guys." Grace smiled as she approached us. "Come in and take a seat in the living room. Can I get you anything to drink?"

"I'm good," I spoke.

"Damien, you look like you could use a drink. Scotch or bourbon?"

"Bourbon. Thanks, Dr. Finn."

Damien and I took a seat on the couch while Grace and Ava sat across from us. Dr. Finn handed Damien his drink.

"London," Dr. Finn spoke. "I firmly believe that I can remove your tumor."

The knot in my stomach intensified as I gave him a nervous smile.

"But it's not going to be easy, and like I said earlier, the risks are very high."

"Dr. Finn, how is it that you are agreeing to do this when all the other doctors said it was impossible?" I asked.

"I don't believe in the impossible, London. If there's a will, there's a way. That's why I've won more awards than all the other doctors." He smirked. "Actually, my daughter, Ava, helped me out with this."

"What?" Damien asked as he looked at Ava.

"My daddy is going to cut away the part of the tumor while she's sitting up. That was my suggestion."

"I'm sorry, but how old are you?" Damien smiled at her.

"I'm seven and I'm a genius. I'm smarter than my parents and I'm going to be a brilliant neurosurgeon like my daddy."

"It's true. She is smarter than me and Grace. Her IQ is off the charts. I've been teaching her about neuro since she could talk."

"My goodness. Thank you, Ava." I smiled at her. "You are definitely going to make a brilliant neurosurgeon one day."

"She's obsessed with brain tumors, thanks to him." Grace rolled her eyes.

"I can do the surgery the day after tomorrow, if that's what you truly want. This is a decision that shouldn't be made lightly, London."

"Will you be able to remove the entire tumor?" I asked.

"Yes. I believe I can. I wouldn't be doing it if I didn't think I could."

"London, why don't you come with me to the kitchen and I'll make us some tea." Grace smiled.

"Can I help, Mommy?"

"Of course you can, sweetie."

Damien

"Another drink?" Dr. Finn asked.

"That would be great. Listen, Dr. Finn, do you in your honest opinion think London should go ahead with the surgery?"

"Let me you ask you the same thing." He handed me my drink. "Do you think she should go through with it?"

"If there's a chance I can be with her for the rest of my life, yes. I love her. I've never loved anyone before, and I never realized how empty my life was until I met her. I run my own company, I'm rich, successful, and I thought I had it all. Turned out, I had nothing."

"I can totally relate to that."

"Don't laugh at me when I tell you this, but I've only known her a little less than a month."

"Hey," he put his hand up, "I barely knew Grace and we ended up married after one drunken night in Vegas."

"Really?" I cocked my head at him.

"Really. You just know, Damien. You just know who your soulmate is regardless of the little time you've known them."

"I'm begging you with my heart and soul to not let anything happen to her," I spoke. "I need that woman in my life."

"I'm going to do everything I can to make sure nothing happens to her. You have my word. But, the one thing I can't guarantee is that she'll come out of all this a hundred percent. So you need to prepare yourself for the aftermath of the surgery. Everyone is different, Damien, and the only thing I can do is remove the tumor and hope for the best."

London and Grace walked back into the room and Grace was holding a little boy in her arms.

"You have two kids?" I asked.

"This is Aiden. He's two years old."

"Is he going to be a neurosurgeon as well?" I smirked at Dr. Finn.

"I'm not sure. I told Grace he can do trauma if she wants him to. But I have this vision of my children being a brilliant brother and sister team."

I glanced over at Grace and she rolled her eyes. I couldn't help but let out a chuckle.

"I'm going to go ahead with the surgery, Dr. Finn," London spoke.

"Okay, London. Come to the hospital tomorrow evening after six. We'll get you admitted, and I'll schedule your surgery for five a.m. the next morning."

A sickness settled inside me as I took hold of her hand and we climbed in the car. She was silent on the way back to the hotel and I didn't want to force her to talk, so I waited until we got back to say something.

"It's a beautiful night. Let's go down to the beach for a while."

"I'm really tired, Damien."

I walked over to where she stood and placed my hand on her cheek.

"We'll bring a blanket, lie on the sand, listen to the ocean, and look up at the stars." I smiled.

The corners of her mouth slightly curved upwards as she nodded her head. I grabbed a blanket that was neatly folded and sitting on a chair and then swooped London up in my arms.

"What are you doing?" She laughed.

"I'm carrying you down to the beach so you don't have to walk." I kissed her lips.

"Damien, people will look at us like we're weird."

"No, baby. People will look at us and say, wow, look at how in love he is with her."

CHAPTER TWENTY-SIX

*L*ondon

For one night, I wanted to forget about Teaghan and the surgery, and Damien made sure I'd done that. We lay on our blanket, my body snuggled against his as his arm wrapped around me. The relaxing sound of the waves crashing against the shore was music to my ears and very calming. When I looked up, the stars illuminated the sky, casting their light down on where we lay.

"Marry me, London," Damien spoke.

"What?" I lightly laughed.

"I'm serious. I want to marry you. I love you, and I know we haven't known each other that long, but it doesn't matter. I know as I take in every breath that I was meant to meet you, love you, and take care of you. You are the love of my life, my star, and my existence. We can get married tomorrow and then after the surgery and when we get back to New York, we'll have a big wedding and celebrate with our friends."

I brought my hand up to his face.

"Yes, Damien Prescott. I will marry you."

"Yes?" He smiled.

"Yes." I laughed.

He brushed his lips against mine and pulled me into him, hugging me so tight, I could barely breathe.

"Where are we getting married?" I asked.

"I don't know. I'll figure that out. Don't you worry about it one bit. I will take care of everything."

❧

*W*hen I awoke, I rolled over to find the empty space beside me. I climbed out of bed, put on my robe, and went into the living area and looked for Damien. But instead, I found a handwritten note with my name on it, leaning up against a silver-covered tray. Opening the envelope, I took out the cream-colored paper and unfolded it. A smile crossed my lips as I read the words he wrote.

Enjoy your breakfast, baby. I had to run some errands.
Here's to our wedding day. I love you.

I poured a cup of coffee and removed the lid from the tray, revealing scrambled eggs, potatoes, a croissant, fresh fruit, and two pancakes with a smiley face on top. As soon as I finished eating, there was a knock on the door. When I opened it, a group of people stood in the hallway, one of them being the hotel manager, Roberto.

"Miss Everly, may we come in?" he asked.

"Yes. Of course."

"We are here to provide you with everything you need for your wedding today. Laura has a selection of dresses for you to pick from. Andre will be doing your hair and makeup. Louise will be doing your nails, and Nico has a tray of wedding bands for you to choose from for your fiancé. When you are ready, I will be back to pick you up."

"Pick me up?"

"Yes. I will be taking you to your wedding."

I couldn't believe Damien did all this, and that this was actually happening. I grabbed my phone and sent him a text message.

"You are the most incredible man I have ever known. Are you coming back?"

"You are the most incredible woman I have ever known. I'm not coming

back until after we're married. It's bad luck to see the bride on her wedding day. I love you, London, and I can't wait to make you my wife."

"I can't wait to make you my husband. I love you too."

I picked a beautiful V-neck sequined, laced, backless form-fitting dress with spaghetti straps. It was light, airy, and elegant. It was the perfect dress for a California wedding. Andre curled my hair and pulled the sides back into an elegant style, surrounding the hairband with small white flowers.

"You look simply gorgeous, Madame." He smiled.

"Thank you." I smiled back.

After picking out Damien's wedding band, Roberto walked in and handed me a bouquet of white calla lilies.

"Your flowers, Miss Everly. Are you ready?"

"I am."

For one day, I had forgotten about everything happening in my life. I never thought I'd live to see my wedding day. I cherished every second that passed, and now, I was about to become Mrs. Damien Prescott. I hooked my arm around Roberto's, and he led me outside to the back of the hotel, where I saw a large archway of flowers and Damien standing underneath it in a black suit.

"Your future husband awaits you." Roberto smiled.

I took in a deep breath and started walking down the white runner that led me to Damien. Once I reached him, he took hold of both my hands as a smile crossed his lips.

"You have taken my breath away. You look stunning."

"So do you, Damien. I love you so much."

"I love you too, baby. Let's do this."

We stood before the minister as he performed our short ceremony. When it was time to exchange rings, I gasped when Damien slipped the large princess-cut diamond on my finger with the matching band. After slipping the ring on his finger, and with tears in my eyes, we were now officially husband and wife.

"You may kiss your bride, Damien," the minister spoke.

He leaned in and brushed his lips against mine as we shared our first kiss as husband and wife.

"Are you ready to go back to the room and celebrate?" he asked.

"Definitely." I smiled.

He picked me up and carried me back into the hotel and up to our room as my arms stayed secured around his neck. We made love, and it was more special than it ever had been. Roberto sent us a beautiful meal, which consisted of lobster and filet, along with a small round cake that was beautifully decorated with pink roses and the words "Congratulations Mr. & Mrs. Prescott."

"We better get dressed. We have to leave for the hospital soon." He softly stroked my cheek.

"I know." I placed my hand on his.

CHAPTER TWENTY-SEVEN

*L*ondon

    We arrived at the hospital where Dr. Finn was waiting for us.

"Guess what, Dr. Finn." I smiled.

"What?"

"Damien and I got married today." I held out my hand.

"Wow. Congratulations." He hugged me and then turned to Damien and shook his hand. "That is wonderful news. I'm sorry you have to spend your wedding night in here."

"It's fine. We already celebrated." Damien smirked.

I signed all the paperwork I needed to, changed into the hospital gown that I'd grown to hate over the years, and climbed into bed, where I was hooked up to an IV.

"Please don't hate me, but I'm going to have to shave part of your head."

"I know, Dr. Finn. This isn't my first time."

He placed his hand on mine and gave it a gentle squeeze.

"I'll see you both at five a.m."

As soon as he walked out of the room, I asked Damien to hand me my camera, for I was going to film a video and post it on my blog. I had thousands of messages from people keeping me in their prayers and wishing me good luck. I expressed my gratitude, and when I was done, I uploaded it and closed my laptop.

"Damien, we never talked about the what if's," I softly spoke.

"There aren't going to be any, London. You're going to pull through this surgery with flying colors."

He climbed into the bed and wrapped his arms around me.

"Everything is going to be fine." He kissed my head. "You're going to be fine."

I lay there, staring at the ring on my finger. Even if I didn't survive the surgery, I at least got to live a day as Mrs. Damien Prescott, and that was something I was incredibly grateful for. But I couldn't help but worry about Damien. I had spent the last year at peace with what was to come, but I wasn't sure if he would ever find peace again if something happened.

*

*T*he nurse came in at four fifteen and woke me up. Damien stirred, kissed the side of my head, climbed out of bed, and went into the bathroom.

"Can you please open my bag and hand me the envelope that is sitting on top?" I asked the nurse.

"Of course." She smiled.

As soon as she handed it to me, I stared at Damien's name, which I had written on the envelope, and then tucked it under my pillow when he emerged from the bathroom.

"I'm sorry, London," the nurse spoke. "But you're going to have to take off your wedding ring."

I stared at it for a moment and then slipped it off my finger, placing it in Damien's palm and closing his fingers around it with tears in my eyes. He took a seat on the edge of the bed, leaned in, and wrapped his arms around me.

"You'll get it back. Do you understand me? You will be wearing this ring again after your surgery," he whispered.

I hugged him tight as the tears freely fell down my face.

"I love you, Damien."

"I love you too."

"Good morning, you two," Jamieson spoke as he stepped inside the room.

He walked over to the bed and placed his hand on mine.

"It's time, London. Are you ready?" he asked.

"Can you give me a minute, please?"

"Of course." He softly smiled.

I pulled the envelope from under my pillow and handed it to Damien.

"What's this?" he asked.

"Just something I wrote to you. I want you to open it after I go into surgery."

"London." Tears filled his eyes.

"It's okay, Damien." I grabbed his hand. "I'm ready, Dr. Finn. Let's go now."

"Come on, people, let's get her to the O.R.," he spoke. "Damien, you can hold her hand and follow us until we get to the doors. Then you can take a seat in the waiting room."

They wheeled me out of the room as my heart raced a mile a minute. Damien held my hand the whole way, and when we reached the doors of the O.R., he leaned down and softly kissed my lips.

"You come back to me. Do not leave me waiting. Do you understand? You come back to me, Mrs. Prescott."

I reached up and placed my hand on his cheek.

"I love you," I whispered.

CHAPTER TWENTY-EIGHT

*D*amien

I watched as the doors opened and they wheeled her inside. When they closed, I stood there with my hands tucked tightly in my pants pockets as fear radiated throughout my body.

"Damien?" Grace softly spoke as she placed her hand on my arm.

I wiped the tears from my eyes and looked at her.

"Come on. Come with me up to the rooftop for a cup of coffee. She's in excellent hands. I promise you that."

I gave her a nod and she led me to the elevator. When the doors opened, we stepped out and over to where the coffee was located.

"How do you take it?" she asked.

"Just black."

She handed me the cup and I took it over to the railing and stared out at the busy city of Los Angeles. I reached in my pocket and pulled out the envelope she had given me.

"She gave me this and told me to open it while she's in surgery. I'm not sure if I want to."

"You have to. It's her wish. Don't let her down by not reading it. I have to go. I'm needed down in the ER. I'll check up on you when I can and I'll go into the O.R. and get updates." She placed her hand on my arm.

"Thanks, Grace. I appreciate it."

She gave me a friendly smile and left the rooftop. I sipped my coffee and stared the envelope I held in my hands. In a way, I already knew what she wanted to say and I couldn't bring myself to open it. I shoved it in my pocket, finished my coffee, and headed down to the chapel. When I entered, I was the only one in there. I took a seat in the first row, folded my hands, and closed my eyes as the tears started to swell. Reality had set in, and no matter how good Dr. Finn was, the risks of this surgery were too high. I needed to be strong for London, and in the process, I became delusional with the fact that she might not survive this. I opened my eyes and wiped my tears as anger flowed through my veins. Just a few short weeks ago, I was a man who didn't care about anything in life except my company. My work made me who I was and validated me. I had become so consumed with making money that I couldn't see what really matter. Until I met London. And now, nothing else mattered but her, and the possibility that I might lose her forever haunted me.

"Why?" I shouted as I looked up. "Why the hell did you bring her into my life? Were you testing me? Is this karma for the way I lived my life and treated people? Is this my punishment? Wasn't it enough for you growing up the way I did? You already punished me by giving me to those horrible people. I was the way I was because of you!" I shouted. "Please." I lowered my head. "London is the best thing that had ever happened to me. I have to feel that I found Dr. Finn for a reason, right? There was no hope for her until she met me. I know you have your hand in our lives, so please do what's right and spare her. Give her back to me so we can live out the rest of our lives together. If you do that, I promise I will never go back to how I used to be. I give you my word."

I pulled out the envelope and opened it. Pulling out the folded piece of paper, I stared at her words.

My dearest husband,

By time you're reading this, I will already be in surgery. I don't know what fate has in store for me, but I need you to make me a promise. If something

happens and I don't make it, I need you to promise me that you'll move on with
your life with your head held high and the memories we made together. I love
you so much and I thank you for loving me. Life will go on without me and I
want nothing more than for you to love your life, even if I am no longer in it. I
want you to take pictures of everything. Tell people that you love them. Do the
things you're scared to do. Those are the little moments in life that matter. Do
those things in memory of me and have no regrets. Promise me, Damien. I will
love you forever. Your wife, London.

I wiped the tears that fell down my face and took in a deep breath. Folding the paper and placing it back in the envelope, I shoved it in my pocket, collected myself, and went up to the surgical waiting room. Only four hours had passed, and as I was sitting there with my face buried in my hands, I heard a voice and felt a hand on my shoulder.

"Damien?"

I looked up and saw Scott standing there. Immediately, I stood up and gave him a hug.

"What are you doing here?" I asked.

"Do you even have to ask? There's no way I was going to let you go through this alone. And don't worry about the company. Everything is really good."

"I'm not worried about it at all. In fact, I could care less right now. Thanks for being here."

"Any update yet?" he asked.

"No."

"Have you eaten anything?"

"No. I can't."

"Damien, you have to eat. You're going to be of no use to London when she gets out of surgery if you're weak. Come on, let's go to the cafeteria. Wait a second, is that a wedding ring on your finger?" he asked in shock.

"Yes." I smiled. "London and I got married yesterday morning."

"Wow, Damien. Congratulations. Why didn't you tell me?"

"Everything happened so fast. I really didn't have a chance."

After we got back from the cafeteria, we took our seats in the waiting room. It was killing me. The waiting and the constant worry and nervousness. As Scott and I were talking, Grace walked in and I stood up.

"I just came from the O.R. Jamieson got to the bottom half of the tumor with no problems. She's stable and everything is going according to plan."

"Thank god." I let out a sigh of relief.

"There's still many more hours to go yet. Just try to relax and I'll keep you updated."

"Thank you, Grace."

She patted my shoulder and walked away.

§.

*I*t felt as if time had stopped. The waiting was excruciating, and I felt like I was losing my mind. I paced back and forth across the waiting room. My heart ached with each minute that passed. I was exhausted, so I sat down in the chair next to Scott and closed my eyes for a few minutes. But it was more than a few minutes.

"Damien?" I heard a voice.

Slowly opening my eyes, I saw Dr. Finn standing over me.

"The surgery went well and London is stable. There were a couple of complications, but nothing to worry about. I've placed her in a medically induced coma until the swelling in her brain goes down and her brain starts to heal."

"How long will that take?" I asked.

"I plan on keeping her that way for about a week, maybe two. It depends. She will be monitored every second."

"Did you get the entire tumor?"

"I did." He smiled. "It was tricky, but I got it. All of it. There is not one speck of that tumor left inside her."

I let out a deep breath.

"Thank you, Dr. Finn." I hugged him.

"Listen, Damien. You need to remember what we talked about. I don't know how she'll be or what kind of deficits she'll have when she wakes up. You need to be prepared for the possibility that she may not be the same woman she was before the surgery."

"It doesn't matter, Dr. Finn. She'll always be the same woman to me, no matter what."

He gave me a sympathetic smile and placed his hand on my shoulder.

"You can go to the ICU and see her. My suggestion would be to check out of Casa Del Mar and get a hotel closer to the hospital."

"I'll do that. Thank you."

"Come on. I'll take you to your wife," he spoke. "And then I'm going to call her doctors and tell them that I removed her inoperable tumor." He smiled.

CHAPTER TWENTY-NINE

*D*amien
       I walked into her room and over to her bedside, where I laid my head on her arm. Her head was covered in a white gauze and she was hooked up to several machines. To see her like this was frightening, but she was here and alive. I stayed with her for a while. I didn't want to leave her side, but I had to check out of Casa Del Mar and find a hotel closer for the remainder of her stay here at the hospital. Scott drove with me to the hotel, where I gathered up all of London's things and my own, packed our suitcases, and drove to the Four Seasons Hotel, where I was able to secure the Royal Suite for the next month, just to be safe.

a

a week had passed, and it was the longest week of my life. I stayed by London's side the entire time, leaving at midnight to go back to the hotel and get some sleep and back to the hospital by six a.m. I occupied my time by working. Dr. Finn said that if I didn't do something, I'd go crazy. I also had Elvis Presley music softly playing for her. Sometimes, I'd come home from the office and she'd have his

music on and sing to me when I stepped off the elevator. It drove me
nuts at first, but now it made me smile. I leaned over and started
singing "Can't Help Falling in Love" to her.

※

A few more days had passed, and Dr. Finn walked into the room.
"The swelling in London's brain is almost gone, so I'm
going to start the process of waking her up. But I want you to know
that it's going to take time for her to come out of it."

"How long?" I asked with concern.

"It could be a couple days or even a week. It's up to her, when she's
ready, and then we'll see what happens." He sighed.

"You sound concerned."

"I am very concerned because I have no way of knowing how she's
going to be."

"Well, whatever happens, happens. We can deal with it. The only
thing that matters is she survived the surgery and she's here."

Dr. Finn took London off the ventilator and started the process of
bringing her out of the coma. I tried desperately to settle the nerves
inside me by picturing the moment she opened her eyes. Another two
days had passed, and she still lay there without any movement. She had
still not woken up.

"Hi," Ava spoke as she walked into the room.

"Ava, what are you doing here?"

"I came to see how London was doing. I overheard my daddy
telling my mommy that he brought her out of the induced coma. She
hasn't woken up yet?"

"No. Not yet."

"It can take several days to weeks. Her brain is in the process of
rewiring and it's going to take some time. She'll wake up when her
brain tells her to."

"You are a very smart little girl. Do your parents know you're up
here?"

"They will once they find out I escaped the daycare center downstairs. This is always the first place they look for me." She grinned.

"You two got married?" she asked as she pointed to my wedding band.

"We did." I smiled. "The day before her surgery."

"Where's her ring?"

"In my pocket for when she wakes up."

"Why wait until she wakes up? You can give it back to her now."

"Ava." Dr. Finn sighed as he walked in. "You know your mother doesn't like it when you escape daycare."

"Sorry, Daddy. I just wanted to come and see how London was doing."

"You're lucky your mother was in the middle of a trauma and they called me. Come on, let's go back downstairs."

"Can I do rounds with you? Please, Daddy," she begged.

A wide smile crossed his lips.

"Okay. You can come with me to see a couple of patients, but then it's back to daycare. And don't tell your mother."

"I won't." She smiled.

I took London's wedding ring out of my pocket and stared at it for a moment. Taking hold of her hand, I slipped the ring on her finger and then brought it up to my lips.

"I love you, baby. Please wake up," I whispered.

I laid my head down on the edge of the bed and I held her hand in mine. Suddenly, I felt her fingers tighten around mine. I lifted my head and she opened her eyes.

"London." I jumped up. "Page Dr. Finn. She's awake," I shouted out the door.

Jamieson came running into the room with Ava in tow.

"London, welcome back. Do you know who I am?" he asked.

She slowly nodded her head.

"Do you know where you are?"

She slowly nodded her head.

"Can you tell me where you are?"

She tried to speak, but the words wouldn't come out.

"Can you squeeze my hand?" he asked her. "Good. Very good."

She struggled to talk, but she couldn't, and I could see the tears swell in her eyes. Ava walked over and lightly grabbed her hand.

"It's okay. Don't be scared. Your brain is still rewiring itself. It's going to take time, but you will be able to speak again."

"Ava, go get a notepad and a pen from the nurses' station."

"Yes, Daddy."

As London lay there, she wouldn't take her eyes off me as the tears streamed down her face.

"You're going to be okay, baby." I reached down and kissed her forehead.

Ava ran back into the room with the notepad and pen and handed it to London.

"London, I want you to tell me how you're feeling," Dr. Finn said.

She slowly wrote on the notepad and showed him.

"Why didn't you just let me die???"

"London, listen to me. I removed the entire tumor. Teaghan is completely gone and she's not coming back. It's going to take time for you to recover from this," he spoke.

She threw the notepad on the floor and looked away from us.

"Ava, go back down to the daycare center now."

"Yes, Daddy." She lowered her head in disappointment.

"Damien, let's step out into the hall. London is confused and angry right now. This type of behavior is common after brain surgery. She may even feel depressed for a while because a part of her is gone. A part of her that had been there for the past fifteen years. Some patients feel it as a type of loss."

"I don't understand," I said.

"It's not for us to understand. She will get through it with your love, patience, and support. As far as her speech, Ava was right that her brain is rewiring, so it's going to take time for it to come back. Just keep talking to her and make her hear your words. So far, if this is the only deficit she has, it's a miracle and can be corrected."

"Thanks, Dr. Finn."

CHAPTER THIRTY

*L*ondon
I was aware of my surroundings. I knew who I was, where I was, and what happened to me. I couldn't vocalize my pain and anguish and I hated every second of it. Damien walked back into the room and I couldn't even look at him because all I saw was the sadness and pain in his eyes. He walked over to the bed and grabbed hold of my hand.

"Look at me, London," he softly spoke.

I wouldn't and just stared out the window.

"Baby, I love you. You're alive. Do you know how happy that makes me?"

I didn't want to hear it because I couldn't say those words back to him.

"Do you want the notepad?" he asked.

I shook my head no and then closed my eyes. Communication ceased to exist between us or anyone, for that fact, over the course of the week. The nurse would come in and get me out of bed to walk, but I couldn't. My legs were so weak that I did nothing but stumble. I hated this and I resented Damien for making me have the fucking surgery in the first place. I was so worried about him that I really didn't stop to think how this would impact me and my life. I was help-less and scared, and I took my anger out on him.

Damien

For three weeks, she took her anger out on me. I tried to go with her when the therapist took her down for physical therapy, but she wouldn't let me. Every time I looked at her, all I saw was anger. I didn't know what to do to help her and Dr. Finn told me that I had to be patient. Patience wasn't one of my strong suits, but for her, I would be, no matter how badly she treated me. I knew the old London was in there somewhere and I was going to get her back, even if I had to fight her.

It was time for us to go back home and I could see the fear in her eyes when Dr. Finn told her. Her legs were getting stronger, but she still had some trouble walking.

"I got in touch with a physical therapist in New York and he's going to be coming to your house three times a week as well as a speech therapist," Dr. Finn spoke. "I'll be in New York next week and I'll stop by to check on you. Also, the two of you are cleared to have sex and as much as you want of it." He smiled. "I'm ordering it as therapy."

She turned her head away from both of us.

I rented a private plane to fly us back to New York. I didn't want her to be amongst all those people on a germ-filled plane. She didn't look at me once the entire flight, but she did write on her notepad when I asked her if she was happy to go home.

"That's not my home," she wrote.

My heart ached when I read that, and I simply dismissed it like all the other things. The car pulled up to the curb of our building, and I climbed out and took London's wheelchair from the trunk. After setting it up, I helped her from the car and into it. As I was wheeling her up to the door, Sammy held it open for us.

"London, it's so good to see you again." He gave her a sympathetic smile.

"She can't speak, Sammy. But she will soon enough." I said.

London wrote down on the notepad and showed it to Sammy.

"It's good to see you too."

Okay, so apparently, the only people she was pissed off at were me and Dr. Finn.

"Sammy, our luggage is in the car. Can you send them up?"

"Of course, Mr. Prescott."

I wheeled her to the elevator, and we took it up to the penthouse. God, it felt so good to be home. I wheeled her into the bedroom and helped her onto the bed.

"Do you want to change into your pajamas?" I asked.

She gave me a dirty look and laid her head down on the pillow and went to sleep. A couple hours later, I went back into the bedroom with a tray of food. The moment I set it down, she took her hand and tossed it off the bed. Anger tore through me and I needed to step away for a moment to collect myself.

ॐ

London

J was struggling. I felt like I fell so deep down the rabbit hole that I would never be able to climb out. Two weeks had passed and all I did was lie in bed. I barely ate and I didn't write two words to Damien. All I did was lie there in a coma-like state, trying to make sense of everything and feeling sorry for myself.

He walked into the room one morning, grabbed some of my clothes from the closet, and tried to dress me.

"We're going out whether you like it or not," he spoke in a stern voice. "I'm taking you for a walk in Central Park."

I immediately grabbed my notepad, and in big, bold letters, I wrote: "NO!" and held it up to him.

"Is that so? Do you really think I'm going to listen? You haven't left this bed once except to go to the bathroom."

I wrote: "NO!" again and shoved the notepad in his face.

"Okay." He walked out of the room, and within moments, he was back with my camera in his hand. "You haven't done shit since you woke up from surgery. You haven't kept up with your blog, nothing. I had to go on there and let everyone know your status because you were flooded with messages from the worried people who have been following you since you started it."

He held up the camera and turned it on.

"Hey, everyone, this is Damien Prescott, London's husband. The reason she hasn't been posting anything is because she's playing the victim. See for yourself." He turned the camera on me. "This is what she's been doing since she woke up from her surgery. She's been feeling sorry for herself and playing the fucking victim."

I leaped at him and knocked the camera out of his hands. In doing that, I fell to the ground. Tears started falling down my face as I tried to scream, but nothing would come out.

"I don't feel sorry for you, London. You're doing this to yourself. I'm trying desperately to help you and you won't let me. What happened to the girl who loved life? Who loved everything about it? What happened to the girl who told me to remember all the little moments and to take my life and make it the best story ever? Where is she?" he shouted.

I looked at my hand that was planted firmly on the floor and stared at my wedding ring. I yanked it off my finger and threw it at him out of anger.

"Oh, so now you don't want to be married to me anymore? Is that what you're telling me? Fine." He reached down and picked up my ring. "Consider this marriage over." He stormed out of the room and left me lying on the floor.

I cried as I dropped completely, rolled on my side, and buried my face in my hands. I heard the elevator doors open and then close. He left and I was all alone. I got myself into my wheelchair and I wheeled myself out into the main area of the house. It was filled with silence and I was completely alone. I wallowed in self-pity as I sat in the middle of the living room. I wheeled myself back to the bedroom and picked up my camera, playing back what he had recorded. I didn't even recognize the woman that was there. I rewound back a little further and found some footage he took when I was in the coma. It was of him singing to me an Elvis Presley song "Can't Help Falling In Love."

"I recorded this so someday when I tell you that I sang to you, you'll believe me," he spoke into the camera.

I slowly closed my eyes as the tears continued to fall. I was so wrapped up in my own emotions that I didn't hear Damien walk in.

"London?" he softly spoke.

I turned my head and stared into his eyes. This was the man I loved with every fiber of my soul. I had let anger overtake me and I couldn't see past the fact that I couldn't speak and could barely walk. I lost sight of who I was. I was tumor free and had the rest of my life to live and I couldn't see that past all the anger. I reached down and picked up the notepad and pen.

"I'm so sorry. I love you, Damien."

"I love you too, baby. We'll get through this. You'll get through this."

He walked over to me, picked me up out of my chair, and held me tight.

CHAPTER THIRTY-ONE

*L*ondon
     He gently laid me on the bed and climbed in next to me,
     pulling me into him. I laid my head on his chest and listened
to his beating heart, a sound that always soothed me. He softly
stroked my hair but didn't say a word. He knew he didn't need to. He
knew all I needed was to be safe in his arms. I sat up and grabbed my
notepad.

"I need sex."

He let out a chuckle. "Seriously? You want to have sex?"

I wrote, "Yes. Right now."

The corners of his mouth curved up into a sexy smile as his fingers
trailed across my lips and over my nightshirt as he traced the outline of
each of my breasts.

"Your wish is my command." His lips brushed against mine.

*T*he next morning, as we were eating breakfast, Damien
     received a phone call from Dr. Finn.

"What did he want?" I wrote down on the notepad.

"He said that a friend of his is stopping by to see you. He said she'll explain who she is when she gets here."

A while later, the intercom rang, and Damien walked over and pressed the button.

"Mr. Prescott, there is someone here to see London. Shall I send her up?"

"Yes, Sammy. Thank you."

Damien and I stood at the elevator and waited for it to come up. When the doors opened, a woman stepped out and introduced herself.

"You must be London." She smiled. "I'm Laurel Coleman and I've heard a lot about you from Jamieson." She extended her hand.

"I'm Damien Prescott, London's husband."

"It's so nice to meet both of you."

"Please, step into the living room. May I offer you something to drink?" Damien asked her.

"I'm fine. Thank you. The reason why I'm here is because I would like you to come to my meditation center. I don't know what Jamieson has told you, but he removed a brain tumor from my frontal lobe a few years back. I had a really hard time adjusting after that surgery, so I took off to Thailand and stayed in a monastery with the monks and learned all about healing the brain and establishing a mind-body connection through meditation. Jamieson told me that you're unable to speak since the surgery, correct?"

I nodded.

"That must be difficult. Even though I didn't experience that, I experienced other things. I thought after I got the tumor removed, I'd be back to normal and life would be grand, but it just seemed things got worse as my brain was healing."

"I can totally relate," I wrote on the notepad.

"Don't worry. I'm going to help you heal your brain." She smiled.

☙

A couple of weeks had passed, and life was returning to normal. My legs were growing stronger every day and I once again was able to walk, only needing to use a cane for when I left the penthouse.

I continued working with my physical therapist, and with Laurel and meditation. Every day and night, I meditated. I didn't give up hope and I knew in time, I'd be able to speak again.

It was a beautiful fall day out and Damien took the day off work and took me to Central Park. We went to Cherry Hill and spread out a blanket on the grass. We had a picnic and watched the people as they went by. The light wind swept across my face as the sun shined down on us. If I hadn't gone through with the surgery, I probably would have been dead by now. Instead, I was tumor free and appreciated the second chance I was given. A deep calmness settled inside me and the anger I had was now gone.

When we got back to the penthouse, I was exhausted. So exhausted I could barely make my way to the bedroom. Damien swept me up in his arms and carried me to the bedroom. After he laid me down, I closed my eyes and slept for a couple of hours. I was awoken by a crash in the kitchen. My eyes opened when I heard Damien yell, "Shit." I climbed out of bed and went to see what happened. When I walked in, I saw the vase that was my mother's lying on the floor in tiny little broken pieces.

"Don't walk in here," he said as he held up his hand.

"Dammit, Damien," I blurted out.

I placed my hand over my mouth and his eyes widened as we stared at each other in shock.

"Did you just say something?"

I swallowed hard and nodded. He walked over to me and firmly gripped my shoulders.

"Say it, baby. Don't nod. Say the word."

"Yes," I softly spoke as he pulled me into an embrace.

"Oh my god. To think that it only took me breaking your mother's favorite vase to get you to speak again."

"It's okay," I slowly spoke.

He broke our embrace and firmly pressed his lips against mine.

"God, I love you so much." He smiled as he placed his forehead on mine.

"I love you," I slowly spoke.

CHAPTER THIRTY-TWO

*D*amien

        Six months had passed, and London's speech was fully recovered. She continued going three times a week to Laurel's meditation center and even managed to get me to go with her. We made it through the toughest times of our lives, and now, we were living each day to the fullest as if it were our last. I cut back on my work schedule. I went into the office at eight and was out by five. Weekends were no longer work days for me because those were the two days I got to spend every minute with my wife. I loved my new life and it wouldn't have been possible had London and I never crossed paths. When I look back on those days of my life, I was a terrible lonely man who only cared about work and making as much money as I could. I never knew the love of one special woman could change me. I didn't think people could change, but I was proof they could. She saw something in me that nobody else had and I would always be grateful for her. She was the love of my life and the only thing I needed in the world.

London

he happiest days of my life were now, and the best days were still to come. My brush with death taught me not to take the little things for granted and to cherish each and every moment we are given. There was a reason Damien and I crossed paths that day in the airport. I was sent to help him, and he was sent to help me. Every morning when I woke up and looked at him, I thanked God for sending him to me. We were meant to heal each other and that was exactly what we did.

We decided not to have another wedding with our friends because the day we were married in California held such special memories for us, that was all we needed. Instead, on the one-year anniversary of our marriage, we would host a big celebration. Not only celebrating our marriage but celebrating the new life I was given. A life full of love, happiness, and free of worry. Damien Prescott once told me that he would never be anyone's knight and shining armor, but he was wrong. He was my knight and shining armor and forever would be.

BOOKS BY SANDI LYNN

If you haven't already done so, please check out my other books. Escape from reality and into the world of romance. I'll take you on a journey of love, pain, heartache and happily ever afters.

Millionaires:

The Forever Series (Forever Black, Forever You, Forever Us, Being Julia, Collin, A Forever Christmas, A Forever Family)

Love, Lust & A Millionaire (Wyatt Brothers, Book 1)

Love, Lust & Liam (Wyatt Brothers, Book 2)

Lie Next To Me (A Millionaire's Love, Book 1)

When I Lie with You (A Millionaire's Love, Book 2)

Then You Happened (Happened Series, Book 1)

Then We Happened (Happened Series, Book 2)

His Proposed Deal

A Love Called Simon

The Seduction of Alex Parker

Something About Lorelei

One Night In London

The Exception

Corporate A$$

A Beautiful Sight

The Negotiation

Defense

Playing The Millionaire

#Delete

Behind His Lies

Carter Grayson (Redemption Series, Book One)

Chase Calloway (Redemption Series, Book Two)

The Interview: New York & Los Angeles Part 1

The Interview: New York & Los Angeles Part 2

Jamieson Finn (Redemption Series, Book Three)

Rewind

One Night In Paris

Second Chance Love:

Remembering You

She Writes Love

Love In Between (Love Series, Book 1)

The Upside of Love (Love Series, Book 2)

Sports:

Lightning

ABOUT THE AUTHOR

Sandi Lynn is a New York Times, USA Today and Wall Street Journal bestselling author who spends all her days writing. She published her first novel, *Forever Black*, in February 2013 and hasn't stopped writing since. Her addictions are shopping, going to the gym, romance novels, coffee, chocolate, margaritas, and giving readers an escape to another world.

Be a part of my tribe and make sure to sign up for my newsletter so you don't miss a Sandi Lynn book again!

Facebook: www.facebook.com/Sandi.Lynn.Author
Twitter: www.twitter.com/SandilynnWriter
Website: www.authorsandilynn.com
Pinterest: www.pinterest.com/sandilynnWriter
Instagram: www.instagram.com/sandilynnauthor
Goodreads: http://bit.ly/2w6tN25
Newsletter: http://bit.ly/2Rz0z2L

22687512R00086

Printed in Great Britain
by Amazon